THE SILENT SECOND

ADVANCE PRAISE

"Just when you thought detective fiction had hit a plateau, along comes *The Silent Second*. Adam Phillips takes us into new territory, running a tight ship, sniffing out LA in detail, and then covering it with a steely patina of darkness in true noir fashion. This taut, smart, fast-paced thriller is from a fresh author to watch."

— Jim Heimann, executive editor at
Taschen America and author of
Sins of the City and *Los Angeles: Portrait of a City*

"*The Silent Second* is *Chinatown* for the Human Resources Department. Full of humor, outrage, and suspense. Adam Phillips's book is everything a thriller should be."

— Phoef Sutton, *New York Times*–bestselling
author of *Heart Attack and Vine*
and *Wicked Charms*

"Beneath the surface of every corporate drone is a story waiting to be told. Adam Phillips solves the mystery hidden in each seemingly innocuous word, mannerism, and expression to expose another piece in this twisting puzzle. Surprising and funny, it turns out this HR professional also makes a damn fine investigator and tells a story that feels honest and fantastic at the same time."

— Sarah Cooper, creator of
TheCooperReview.com and author of
100 Tricks to Appear Smart in Meetings

THE SILENT SECOND

A CHUCK RESTIC MYSTERY

Adam Walker Phillips

PROSPECT
·PARK·
BOOKS

Published by Prospect Park Books
2359 Lincoln Avenue
Altadena, California 91001
www.prospectparkbooks.com

Distributed by Consortium Book Sales & Distribution
www.cbsd.com

Library of Congress Cataloging-in-Publication Data
Names: Phillips, Adam Walker, 1971- author.
Title: The silent second : a Chuck Restic mystery / by Adam Walker Phillips.
Description: Altadena, California : Prospect Park Books, 2017.
Identifiers: LCCN 2016053803 (print) | LCCN 2017012183 (ebook) | ISBN 9781945551055 (ebook) | ISBN 9781945551048 (paperback)
Subjects: LCSH: Murder--Investigation--Fiction. | Self-actualization (Psychology)--Fiction. | Private investigators--Fiction. | BISAC: FICTION / Mystery & Detective / General.
Classification: LCC PS3616.H4475 (ebook) | LCC PS3616.H4475 S55 2017 (print) | DDC 813/.6--dc23
LC record available at https://lccn.loc.gov/2016053803

Cover design by Nancy Nimoy
Book layout and design by Amy Inouye, Future Studio
Printed in the United States of America

For Olivia

MAMBA FOR MEN

My first and only interaction with Ed Vadaresian was over an excessive-cologne complaint. An administrative assistant and mother-to-be on the thirty-second floor was unable to complete her daily functions because of debilitating headaches she suffered throughout the day. She attributed the headaches to a heightened sense of smell brought about by her pregnancy, and to the overwhelming scent of Mr. Vadaresian's cologne. It appeared that his simply walking past her cubicle sent her reeling with sharp pains behind her left eye for which the only respite was a long nap in the darkened back seat of her Subaru.

The complaint was quickly escalated to my desk after an initial review warranted involvement from senior management. The administrative assistant had hit the trifecta for trial lawyers: lesbian, African American, and over forty. Throw in pregnant and she attained a legendary superfecta status, which most HR executives never witness in their entire careers.

The administrative assistant was well known to our department. In her brief four-year career she had lodged a total of seven complaints, including the one against Ed. They ranged from the ludicrous (serving Aunt Jemima syrup at the annual pancake social was a direct assault on her as a woman of color) to the extremely ludicrous (a request to eradicate the phrase "low-hanging fruit" from our lexicon as it was offensive to women of a certain age). She also had an issue with tardiness, failed to meet many of her deadlines, and overall was a consistently inconsistent performer. All of this, however, was irrelevant when it came to the complaint that she lodged against Ed.

Human Resources exists not as a "resource" for associates (the term "employee" was eradicated decades ago from corporate offices) but as a way for corporations to limit exposure to lawsuits. The majority of programs, counseling, and conflict resolution services all worked toward a single goal: avoid getting sued. A decade ago I unveiled a new concept at the company called the "Mother's Room" (it was renamed "Resting Room" after a complaint by a single-parent dad). This was a dedicated room on every floor where a mom could go to relax, or if she was breast-feeding, to pump milk in private. Each room contained a small cot, a mini-fridge for the milk, and a phone in case of emergency. Publicly, we wanted to encourage a healthy work/life balance and smooth the difficult transition from having a child to returning to work. Privately, we witnessed an alarming spike in maternity-fueled legal actions and figured the costs of maintaining a seven-by-five room with an Army cot paled in comparison to the cost of attorney fees and cash settlements on unhealthy workplace lawsuits. There is no justice in Corporate America, only the lens of the liability framework.

So when the excessive-cologne complaint was lodged by a low-performing associate with a history of mental instability against an associate who had a long, respected track record of adding value to the company, we had no choice but to bring Ed Vadaresian in for some feedback.

"Have a seat, Ed," I said, leading him to the little, round table in my office. I closed the door to give us some privacy but immediately regretted it. The combination of bergamot orange and myrrh with a healthy dash of gasoline was lethal on the nasal cavity. The first thing I noticed was a dull, numbing sensation high up in my nose between my eyes. I got the light-headed swirls of a nonsmoker taking his first drag.

"Am I in trouble?" he asked.

"No, you're not in trouble," I told him as my eyes began to water. "There's an issue that's been brought to our attention that we need to clear the air on."

But before I could launch into it, he started to cry. His shoulders heaved as he tried to compose himself. Attempts to breathe sputtered into short gasps for air.

Ed was in his early fifties though he looked younger. Like a lot of Armenians he was in that "forever forty" camp of men that age early but reach a form of stasis and they seemingly stop getting older. Ed worked in our Office Services division, which was a catchall group that handled everything from mail delivery to ergonomic evaluations. He was a workhorse who still lived by the old adage of hard work and respect for the people who pay you. He hadn't realized yet that he was more valuable to the company than the company was to him.

"It's about the Mother's Room, isn't it?" he blurted out. "That nice Chinese lady—"

"Asian American," I corrected.

"—on thirty-two saw me come out yesterday. I only used the phone once because I left my cell at home." He rubbed his eyes with one of his thick fingers. "I promise I won't do it again, Mr. Restic."

The unnecessary formality of addressing me as "mister" even though I was younger than him telegraphed the fear behind the promise. Associates had good reason to distrust Human Resources. A simple word like "issue" could be the death knell of a career. One minute you are chatting about this non-event, and two weeks later you have a case built against you. Some Tuesday before noon you receive an unexpected "Got a sec?" call, and suddenly you are down in HR signing papers that seal your termination. In a job that had few redeeming aspects, this was among the worst.

My co-manager and office neighbor, Paul Darbin, relished it. He'd linger on phrases such as "not meeting expectations" to give them the gravitas of a life sentence. He sometimes paced behind a seated associate like he was a Stasi interrogator. When interviewing associates over a complaint, he'd wait until they finished talking before slowly, and very deliberately, writing a note on his pad that he'd cover with his other hand. One time I snuck a peak at his notebook and discovered he was writing out his grocery list.

"This isn't about the phone in the Mother's Room," I told him, though the thought of the original complainer stumbling upon Ed as she tried to use the special room was enough to make me think it should be.

"It's not?"

"No. We've received a complaint that I want to talk over with you."

"What kind of complaint?" he asked with trepidation. "About my work?"

"No, not your work," I said and realized how incredibly inane this whole thing was. A man who had done nothing wrong now had to be humiliated with all the formality of a federal deposition. Protocol dictated I document everything, including the Mother's Room phone admission, but I cast it all aside and just told him the truth.

"Ed, you're wearing too much cologne."

He looked legitimately befuddled. "Someone complained about my cologne? Why would they do that?"

"Well, for one it's an awful scent. Two, the person who complained might be certifiably insane." The latter comment was reckless and undoubtedly would come back to haunt me but it had been brewing for years. I was starting to verbalize what I had questioned all along—there was so little worth to a life spent avoiding lawsuits.

"You really don't like it?"

"Ed, I'm telling you that stuff is awful. What's it called?"

"Mamba for Men," he answered, and the image of a white-fanged cobra coiled around a twisting bottle sprang to mind. "The young lady at the counter said it was perfect on me."

"They get paid to lie," I explained. "How many

spritzes do you use in the morning? And be honest."

"Two," he laughed, which meant five.

"Okay, make it a half spritz and we should be fine."

He nodded, but I could see something else was on his mind. "About the phone in the—"

"I didn't hear anything, Ed," I said as I led him to the door and welcomed the fresh air from the hallway. Ed turned to me and shook my hand, ever the professional. "You're a good man, Mr. Restic."

"No, I'm not," I said. "But I'm trying."

Two weeks later, the man who never called in sick, who several times a year was forced to take time off when he hit his maximum accrual of vacation days, didn't show up to work. One unexcused absence turned into two, then a week's worth, and Ed Vadaresian was officially declared a missing person.

THE JEWEL CITY

Corporations have a regenerative quality that allows them to adapt to any internal disruptions, and as such, Ed's duties were seamlessly absorbed by other associates with nary a hiccup. Once again the myth that "this place will miss me when I'm gone" was dispelled. Policy dictated that Ed's unused vacation days were drained before being placed on leave without pay, which was partially subsidized by the state of California. That ran out after two and a half months, and Ed Vadaresian was summarily removed from our books.

When I learned of Ed's termination, I decided to break from policy and personally deliver his belongings to his family. It seemed unnecessarily callous to mail a trove of his effects to loved ones still searching for answers. But I had another reason to take the drive out to Glendale.

I'd begun to fear the weekend. While most associates counted off days like cartoon prisoners—"Three more days till Friday!"—I viewed the approaching two days off with particular dread. It all started with my separation from Claire. Without the distractions of meaningless office tasks, I was left to ponder how it all fell apart. Dropping off Ed's belongings provided at least a short respite from that inevitable contemplation of a failed marriage, after which I could never come up with an explanation.

I grabbed several boxes and headed down to Ed's floor. A fifteen-year career at the same desk can generate quite a lot of stuff, and I anticipated hoarding levels of accumulation—folders of corporate memos that had never been read, a fifty-photograph collage of newborn twins, enough potted bamboo plants to open a kiosk in Chinatown. But Ed's desk was remarkably sparse. He had few personal items, and those he had lacked anything remotely unique to him. There were fifteen years' worth of corporate appreciation—all crystal, all from Tiffany, all engraved with his name and anniversary year. Other than that, there was a pile of non-work-related paperwork and an extra brown belt I assumed was for those days when he forgot to wear one. All of his belongings fit comfortably in a standard file box.

I walked to the elevator lobby with the contents tucked under my arm. I was growing unnecessarily morose carrying the accumulation of a man's career in such a small box when my co-manager Paul came sauntering into the lobby.

"Hey Chuck, what you got there?"

Paul kept a ponytail but none of the ideals of the counterculture. Like a lot of other ex-hippies, he seemed more interested in telling everyone else what they were doing wrong than actually living what he preached.

"I'm going to drop Ed Vadaresian's belongings off to his family," I told him.

"That's cool," he said as the elevator chimed and we stepped in. "Who's Ed again?"

Until you learned the shortcuts in Los Angeles, you never felt like you belonged. I took surface streets out of downtown and avoided the freeway rush hour at its usual crawl. I sped around Dodger Stadium through Elysian Park, and came up the back way along the LA River. I crossed over one of the concrete bridges and wound my way into Glendale.

The city was one long, sloping hill from the lowlands of the LA River basin to the top of the San Gabriel foothills. Once a bastion of white Protestants, Glendale transformed drastically over the course of the last fifty years. The city's immigrants settled into neat little rows like a cross-section of the earth's strata exposing millennia of climate change. At the bottom were dark swaths of newly arrived Central Americans, which quickly gave way to soft patches of Filipinos and then Persians. As you moved farther up the hill you hit a broad stretch of Armenians crammed into the tiny houses and apartment complexes near the downtown. At the very top perched a rarefied group in the foothills, where the air was thinner and the skin several shades lighter.

When I came to Los Angeles some twenty years ago, I settled in Glendale for the cheap rent and proximity to my office downtown. Everyone assumed I was Armenian because I lived there. Correcting them was inevitably followed by the question, "Why would you live in

Glendale if you didn't have to?"

Ed's house was on one of the flat, grid-like streets that slashed through the area south of the freeway. The house itself sat in perpetual shadow from the large apartment complex next door. I parked my car among a sea of late-model luxury sedans that didn't align with the less-than-modest neighborhood.

There were several Armenian teenagers in overly de-signed shirts milling about on Ed's front porch. Fashion and grooming took an unusually high priority among the younger generation of Armenian men. They tended to have an effete obsession with appearance that re-sulted in entire days spent at the gym, the nail salon, and the mall.

I grabbed the box of Ed's belongings out of my trunk and headed up the concrete walk. I scanned the group and tried to figure out which one was Ed's son. I didn't have much time to guess because as soon as they saw me approaching they scattered like mercury from a broken thermometer. No one ran—they all just glided away. The only one left was a thinner, hairier version of Ed, who also shared his father's predilection for too much cologne.

"Are you Ed's son?" I asked.

He pretended like I wasn't there.

"I'm Chuck," I said, extending my hand.

The boy eventually shook it but he couldn't be both-ered to actually turn and face me to do it.

"Rafi," he said, staring out at the street.

"I work with your father," I said, purposely using the present tense. "I spoke to someone on the phone about dropping off some of your dad's belongings."

"That's nice of you," he replied, but he didn't actually mean it.

"I hope…" I started, choosing my words carefully, "I hope everything's okay with your dad."

"Why wouldn't it be?"

From the frustration in Rafi's voice, it didn't sound like the family had learned anything more about Ed's disappearance.

"Should I just leave these here?" I asked, gesturing to the box.

"Give them to Papik," he said. He leaned back in his chair and shut his eyes as if settling in for a late afternoon nap.

Not knowing whom he was talking about or how to find this Papik, I settled in on the railing and waited. I soon found myself studying Rafi's shirt, a dizzying design of vines, skulls, and celestial bodies that, if you stared hard enough and long enough, mutated into a fourth image while giving you a headache.

Rafi opened one of his eyes, checking to see if I'd left.

"Still here," I said.

He reluctantly pulled himself to his feet and beckoned me to follow him inside. It was a tight, two-bedroom bungalow with a standard layout. It felt more accommodation than home, underscored by the fact that the entire interior was covered in cheap tile, making for easy cleanup when preparing for the next set of nameless occupants.

"My father probably got a deal on a bulk order," Rafi said about the tile.

The house also lacked any traces of femininity. There'd been no mention of a mother, and I began to wonder if she existed. Even without her, the simple math of rooms versus occupants highlighted a common fact about many immigrant households—rarely did anyone get a room to themselves.

The image that Rafi gave off on the outside—with the luxury cars and designer clothes and twenty-dollar manicures—didn't match the reality at home, that old-world tradition in which the family sticks together, one's thoughts were everyone's thoughts, and there was always a line for the bathroom.

"He's out there," Rafi said, swinging open the back door and pointing to a swirl of smoke rising from the detached garage.

I stepped down into the yard but turned back.

"Rafi, if there's anything we can do—"

"You want to help?" he interjected.

"If I can," I said, wary of what was coming next.

He just laughed and spared me whatever caustic remark he had stored up.

I followed the smoke past a row of lemon trees to a gate that led out into the alley where an old man was hunched over a grill laid out with peppers on metal skewers long enough that they could be props in a sword-swallower act.

"Smells great," I said and introduced myself.

He immediately took my icebreaker and ran with it by launching into a long discourse on the art of grilling peppers. You want to blister but not burn. A paper bag to steam the skin off. Leave the seeds inside if you want your face melted. Somewhere in the middle of the tutorial he noticed the box under my arm and the air went out of him. He continued to talk about the peppers but even to him they were just words.

"My daughter wasn't the prettiest," the old man confessed, "but she was still a beautiful girl." This kind of reflection saved for eulogies seemed to confirm my suspicion that Rafi's mom wasn't around anymore. "Good thing she got most of her mother's looks and not all of mine," he joked. "We came here forty years ago, but not Glendale. We lived in Hollywood with the other Armenians but we are all here now. What do you think of the house?"

"It's nice."

"It should be nicer," he said with little self-pity. If anything, there was resentment in his voice. I scanned the garage, which served as an extra living room rather than a place to park your car. There was more character in this little space than the entire house and you got the sense that this was where he spent most of his day.

"My daughter wanted to live up on the hill, not down here." He gestured toward the looming San Gabriel foothills where a thousand California ranches twinkled in the late afternoon sun, staring down at him, smiling. "She was the dreamer. All the boys in the old neighborhood wanted to know her. But she only liked Bedros."

He said the name like it was a curse. It was quiet for a few moments, save for the dying hiss of the peppers on the grill. The old man fiddled with the peppers, readjusted the coals, did anything to not talk about Bedros. I recalled Ed's personnel file where associates list out legal names and aliases. Bedros was Ed's given name.

The old man reminded me of another Armenian who lived across from me when I first came to Glendale. One day he bought a brand-new Cadillac that he couldn't afford. For the older generation of immigrants, the American dream still included chrome and a hood ornament. This car had none of that but the emblem was there and of course the iconic name. The old man rushed over to my yard to be congratulated on his purchase. He had a father's pride with that car. But it was short-lived, for as soon as he entered the house, his wife tore into him. His two grown sons soon descended on the scene. They eventually took the car back to the dealer and begged him for what little down payment was given. The old man was too ashamed to mention the Cadillac again. The way Ed's father-in-law sulked over his peppers made me think he was ashamed, too. Not for a returned car, but for how his daughter's life had turned out.

"Then he leaves me like this, with this house, that boy...." He let the words trail off.

"What do you think happened to Ed?" I asked.

"I don't know. One of his business things."

"Was he doing something on the side?" I asked.

"He's Armenian," he said with a laugh. "Everyone's got something on the side."

"Have the police told you anything?"

He waved my question off. "They don't care about us," he said. "They don't even talk to us anymore."

For some reason, curiosity maybe, I asked him for the detective's name and immediately regretted it. He scurried over to a workbench and produced a business card from an old box.

"Will you try and help us?" he asked eagerly.

"I don't know what I can do," I told him truthfully.

"More than what the police are doing."

"You're better off working with them. Or if they aren't doing enough, hire a private detective—"

"With what money?" he dismissed. "Bedros has all the money but we can't use it."

"I'm not following."

"Look at this house he made my daughter live in," he said. "He never spent a penny on her. You should have seen the wedding. It was so cheap. Armenians like to throw a good party—the food, the wine, the cakes. I was embarrassed for my girl."

I couldn't distinguish the truth from resentment toward a son-in-law he didn't like. Ed earned a modest salary, but I also knew the powerful combination of a committed tightwad and compounding interest. Plus what he had going on the side, whatever that amounted to. Ed the missing person became more intriguing the more I learned about him.

But a long career in HR was telling me to disengage. A whole FTE (full-time employment) can be lost in the minutiae of lives of people you hardly know. There were deep issues within this family, as there always are, and it was time to return this discussion to a more formal level. The policy of mailing a former associate's personal effects was looking more appealing by the minute.

"Please, sir," he pleaded. "We need help."

I retreated into corporatespeak.

"Let me consider it," I told him, which he enthusiastically accepted, pumping my hand graciously. The old man was so little versed in conference-room jargon that he failed to realize that phrase was as close to a definitive "no" as one would get.

HOOK NOSE

I looped around the side of the house under an un-
kempt hedge of bougainvillea and headed back to my
car. I heard voices as I came up on the front porch
where Rafi and a man were deep in conversation, speaking in hushed tones. Rafi was doing most of the talking
while the other man leaned calmly on one of the rail-
ings. He was quite a bit older than Ed's son and wasn't
from the original set I encountered when I first arrived
at the house. He spurned the designer T-shirts and jeans
for a plain pullover and black pants. He spoke very little
but when he did it was forceful enough that Rafi clipped
short whatever he was saying. They didn't notice me
until I emerged from the overgrown brush. I was able
to get a clear look at the man's profile, which was dom-
inated by an unnaturally angular nose, possibly indicat-
ing it had been broken several times.

"Take care, Rafi," I said and crossed the lawn to my
car. Out of the corner of my eye I caught a shared look
between Rafi and the new man on the porch. There was
an awkward silence before I got a reply.

"Hold on a sec," Rafi shouted and jogged over to me. I glanced back at the porch where the man was still sitting on the rail, his back to us, like he wanted to avoid being seen.

"Did you get to talk to my grandfather?" he asked, though I wasn't sure what he thought I was doing the last ten minutes in the garage if not talking with him.

"Yes, we spoke."

"I should have given you a heads-up before you went out there. He can be a little hard to deal with."

"I'm not following you."

"What did you guys talk about? I mean, did you talk about my dad?"

He was probing, poorly.

"Sure, we talked about your dad," I answered, purposely keeping my reply short and devoid of detail.

"That's cool. Did he, did he ask you for help?"

"Well, like I told you earlier, any help we can provide, just feel free to ask." I knew that wasn't what he was asking but wanted to string him along. He had that look of a child who thinks he is being clever by pulling one over on you, but the maneuvers are clunky and obvious.

"What about helping to find my dad? Did he bring that up at all?"

"Yes, he mentioned that."

"And are you? Are you going to help?" Rafi asked the question in a way that sounded like he wanted an affirmative reply, but his body language told me he didn't want anything to do with me looking for his father.

"No," I told the truth. "There's nothing I can do that the police aren't already doing."

Relief immediately spread over him like a deep exhale. He looked much more at ease and proved it by becoming overly chatty.

"That's what I told him but he never listens. I love the guy, don't get me wrong, but he can be pretty hard to deal with. He's crazy like that," he explained. "I bet he talked about my mom, right? Some stuff about coming to the States and living in Hollywood like it was a palace or something," he laughed. "That guy's living in a fantasy world."

"What happened to your mom, Rafi, if you don't mind me asking?"

"She was a drunk," he said coldly. There was pain in his voice, but he spoke with a half-smile. "She crashed her car and died when I was thirteen. She wasn't even drunk at the time."

"I'm sorry."

"Does that sound like the same person my grandfather talked about?" he challenged.

We stood there in silence while Rafi worked to shove the thoughts about his mother back into the compartment they came from. "Anyway," he said, "thanks for bringing my dad's stuff out. I'll let him know."

"What do you mean?" I asked. "Have you spoken to your father?"

"Sure," he replied casually.

"When?"

"Last week."

"What happened? Where is he?"

"He's not here. He's back in Armenia."

"Is he okay?"

"Yeah, he's fine," Rafi assured. "He just had some

stuff to take care of back home."

"Why didn't he tell anyone? I mean, your grandfather is worried. We are all worried."

"I bet he's worried," he said with a laugh.

"Listen, the next time you talk to your father tell him to call me. Better yet, tell him to call the police. This is very serious."

"Okay, I'll tell him," he agreed as he took my business card.

"I mean that, Rafi."

"I understand."

I turned and walked to my car. I was fairly certain Rafi was lying about his father being in Armenia, but why he did it was a mystery. The Vadaresians were a strange and complex family, and I had merely scratched the surface of their lives.

As I got into my car, I glanced over the roof at Rafi, who was back on the porch talking to the hook-nosed man. They seemed to have resumed their earlier conversation. The man still hadn't turned in my direction.

I took the freeway back against the grain of traffic. I approached the interchange below Dodger Stadium and eased into the left lane that slipped over the river in the direction of my apartment. A sudden pit formed in my stomach as I pictured myself in my apartment, alone, with nothing to do and several hours to go before the welcome distraction of a night's worth of sleep. Those were the hours I feared the most, when I had nothing but my own thoughts. At the last second, I jerked right and took the route back to the office. Despite my initial rule of disengagement, there was more I wanted to learn about Ed.

RED ZONE

The skyscraper had a funereal quality once the cleaning crews had filtered out. Even the boldly ambitious had realized there was no point in staying late on a Friday if no one was there to witness their dedication. I padded down the empty hallway as the sensor-triggered lights flicked on to guide my way. The hum of the white-noise maker was unnervingly loud without the office chatter and keyboard clacking it was supposed to mask.

While I waited for my computer to boot up, I pulled out the card Ed's father had given me. The old man was skeptical that the police would find his son-in-law, and I tended to agree with him. From my short time living in Glendale, I had learned that the police force there was more of a revenue-generating unit than a crime-solving one.

In that pursuit they employed myriad schemes to catch drivers in minor, but extremely costly, infractions. DUI checkpoints were primarily used to nab drivers with expired tags. One nefarious scheme involved an old lady whom they paid to use a crosswalk on an extremely busy street. If a driver entered said crosswalk before the woman had both feet back on the sidewalk, the officer would emerge from his hiding place and inform the driver of the bad news. They made the woman walk back and forth for hours, and the longer she was out there, the longer it took for her to get across, and the thinner the patience of the driver waiting for her. It was a very lucrative operation.

I read the name on the card—Aricelli Alvarado. The fact that there was a Latino on the force wasn't too surprising. Glendale PD was made up mostly of Caucasian males with overly crisp uniforms and buzz cuts, but it had its share of Latinos and Asians who commuted up from Alhambra. One group rarely represented was Armenians, a result seemingly by choice on the part of the police force and the potential applicants.

I dialed the number and eventually got a recording of a woman's voice. As the message wound down I panicked and hung up. I had no clue what I was going to say. *Hi, I am a nobody who works in HR where a missing guy used to work, and I want to check up on how the investigation is going.* She would probably think I was a crank. At worst, she'd get suspicious that I was somehow involved. I once read that serial killers like to know the details of the investigation into their murders. I realized, however, that she now had my number as a missed call with no message, and I was forced to call her back and leave a brief one. Already I was looking suspicious.

I pulled up Ed's digital file from our system. He came to the United States in 1980 and became a naturalized citizen in 1988. He had no formal education but was able to pass a high school equivalency exam. Background checks uncovered nothing of significance.

He was involved in a legal dispute in the 1990s but the sides settled amicably. Ed had zero presence on the standard social networking sites and therefore could not be profiled for potential issues, such as a propensity to do tequila shots out of a stripper's belly button. He was widowed and had one son. He named his father-in-law as his sole beneficiary.

As an investment company that traded in securities, under law we were required to monitor associate transactions for conflicts of interest and insider trading. The majority of associates didn't dabble in stocks or real estate and thus had nothing to report, but Ed's entry was quite full. Maybe his father's suspicion of a vast, secret fortune was accurate.

Ed owned four properties in all. The first was the home I visited in Glendale, which he bought back in 1998, a good five years before the housing bubble took its first puff. Two other properties looked to be rental units in Glassell Park, and the fourth was in an industrial section not far from my apartment. Ed was a shining example of what drove Los Angeles.

While the entertainment industry was the face of the city, property was the heart that gave it life. One had to look no further than the names of the various art and music venues around the city serving as the vanity plates of the extremely wealthy. From the Mark Taper Forum to the Ahmanson Theatre, the men who built Los Angeles's cultural scene did it on the backs of the real estate and development business. Land was Los Angeles. What was unclear, however, was how the name Ed Vadaresian with his $68,000 salary was able to join the junior ranks of such an exclusive club.

I called up the real estate agent my wife and I used on our two previous homes. I wanted to learn more about these properties that Ed owned, particularly the financial situation with them.

"Are you by chance looking to buy?" she asked in a playful way that failed to mask the desperation in her voice. I thought I heard her lick her lips.

"Just looking for some information on a couple of properties," I answered without answering her question. "I believe they are all owned by the same individual."

"Look at you," she laughed, "swooping in on some distressed opportunities, are you?"

"Could be," I said.

"Cash is king, you know."

"Cash *is* king," I replied.

"You're smart to buy and not rent," she said. "Did you know the median mortgage payment just fell below the average rent on a comparable home?"

It was an innocuous enough comment but in it was a troubling development. She assumed I was looking for a place to occupy as opposed to a place to generate income. Why would she assume that a person who, as far as she knew, lived in a house in the Hollywood Hills with his wife be looking for a new place to live unless someone had told her that Claire and I had separated? So Claire was openly talking about our separation with others.

"Do you have a pen?" I snapped. I gave her the addresses of the properties Ed owned.

"Hmm," she said, "I'm not too familiar with those streets." That wasn't much of a surprise as she specialized in homes with private gates, not grates on the windows. Glassell Park was a run-down area tucked under Glendale and known widely for its gang violence. Los Angeles police had taken a containment policy on the neighborhood. They tacitly allowed the criminal activity to work itself out as long as it didn't migrate up the hill to Mount Washington and its city-view homes.

"They're in some up-and-coming areas," I said.

"You know, since you mentioned it, I have an open house tomorrow for this great house near Hillhurst, south of Sunset. I think it's perfect for you."

"South of Sunset, huh?" I repeated only because I knew it would annoy her. In her heyday she would never have worked that far down the hill on the crappier end of Koreatown. The financial crash and halting recovery winnowed out the winners and losers in the real estate world. It sounded like she was a member of the latter.

"Oh, don't worry," she told me. "It's still a good ways from Kimchi-Land. Come by tomorrow!"

"Red Zone!" I shouted, but she hung up too quickly.

I laughed at how naturally that phrase slipped from my mouth. "Red Zone" was the high-water mark of a career I didn't so much choose as rise up with, like a skiff in the tide. When I joined the firm I was just a kid out of college looking for a paycheck. They started me doing administrative work in the personnel division. Only later would it be renamed "Human Resources." My first job was to collect and destroy all the ashtrays in the office. The state of California had recently banned smoking in the workplace, and being the new guy, I was chosen to be the messenger bearing bad news. Leather-faced administrative assistants glared at me as I wheeled my cart through the office. We established a smoking room on one of the floors but even that was eventually closed after a series of secondhand smoke lawsuits. Eventually everyone had to go outside and huddle in a roped-off area far from the building's entrance.

As corporate litigations rose, along with the sizeable compensation that juries were awarding, companies across the country scrambled for ways to mitigate the risk of being sued. I found a niche where one didn't exist before—liability eradication. My big breakthrough came in 1993.

The hot issue of the day was sexual harassment, following the Navy Tailhook scandal. A pat on the ass, a couple "sweet cheeks" comments, and a promotion awarded to a male colleague could turn into a slam-dunk case. We quickly realized that changing associate behavior would take time, especially among the older set of associates who still expected their "secretaries" to buy gifts for their wives *and* their girlfriends. We were ripe for lawsuits.

Like many discoveries in Los Angeles, my aha moment came while sitting in traffic. That's where I devised the "Stoplight System." It was a way for associates to warn each other that their words or actions were inappropriate. It worked like this.

There were three zones: Red, Yellow, and Green. Green was logically the safest zone; yellow meant you were approaching a dangerous area; and red was purely unacceptable behavior. So say someone was to ask an African American associate about his plans for the holidays.

"What are you doing for Christmas, Gary?"

This could be countered with a warning that the seemingly innocuous question wasn't entirely appropriate.

"*Yellow Zone, Jerry,*" he would say. "*My family chooses to celebrate Kwanzaa at this time of year.*"

If the dialogue were to escalate—"*You know that's a made-up holiday, right?*"—all the offended party had to say were two words—"*Red Zone*"—to alert everyone of the seriousness of the offense. The issue would then immediately be reported to Human Resources.

The beauty of the Stoplight System was that it put the onus of educating the workforce on the offended party. It also hedged against claims that the company willingly ignored signs of discrimination. After all, it was on the complainant to notify in the moment if there was an issue and then file it with the appropriate department. A person could not later claim habitual abuse if he or she failed to follow the policies set by the system.

The program was a huge success. We never had to pay out an unsafe workplace claim. It also launched me into management. I never quite replicated the success of the Stoplight System, but that didn't matter. Reputations are built on first impressions and they last for many years. I parlayed my reputation into numerous promotions and an outer office on the north side of the building. I achieved a level of success at which I could soon throttle back on my career journey and begin the long, slow descent into early retirement. That is, of course, unless I ruined it by foolish actions like snooping through personnel files after everyone had gone home for the weekend.

Although the family had asked me for help, sifting through someone's personnel file was in direct violation of our ethics policy. It was another poor decision I made, one that no more than a year ago would have been unthinkable.

I didn't want to admit it, but I had changed since my separation. The enthusiastic dedication of a mid-level corporate cog was eroding to a point where I was putting my long-term future with the company in jeopardy. All those creeping doubts about the value of a career in liability management surfaced in my comments in meetings. They were caustic, not yet poisonous, but the shift was palpable. I needed to be more careful. Even the hatchet man has a hatchet with his name on it waiting to fall.

As I reflected on my mistakes, I noticed something at the top of Ed's file that made my heart skip. There was a small call-out box that listed all the people who had viewed the file. There was my name alongside today's date stamp. This tool was put in place to monitor ethics violations like the one I was committing. If anyone were to look through this file they would see I had been snooping. That was a very unlikely scenario and one I could easily talk my way out of but the threat was there.

Then I noticed something else—I wasn't the only one nosing around Ed's file. Right above my name was that of my co-manager, Paul Darbin. I pondered this discovery for a moment. Ed wasn't in Paul's coverage group so he had no work-related reason to look at his file. Also, by his comment earlier in the day by the elevators, it seemed he didn't even know who Ed was. It was odd that he would say that when he had viewed the man's profile just two days earlier.

ARMENIAN POWER

As financial pundits desperately searched for signs of a recovery from the 2007 crash, the catchphrase "green shoots" seeped into their daily lexicon. They pointed to any economic report that was even remotely positive as an indication of good tidings ahead. These wonderfully delicate seedlings were emerging from the rubble, signifying rejuvenation and future prosperity. Humans can be relentlessly optimistic when they need to be. One area that didn't need to believe in green shoots was Hancock Park.

I drove through the tiny streets with their Colonial Revivals and sprawling lawns on my way to meet the broker who had worked with Ed on a recent deal. Business really was soft with my old real estate agent because she got back to me with this information within the hour. Ed was underwater on the two apartment complexes in Glassell Park. The situation on the Lincoln Heights property was bleaker as he hadn't made a payment in over a year. He had tried to sell the property weeks before he disappeared but for some reason it had fallen out of escrow.

The broker's office was in Larchmont Village, a one-block area serving as the mini-downtown for Hancock Park. It specialized in brunch and Pilates. Saturday afternoon was its high season so I was forced to park at one of the meters on a side street.

Emerald Properties occupied the space over a fine wine and cheese shop. The company was allowed one of the ground-floor bays to advertise its services, but the actual office was up a creaky flight of stairs. Like cars, you couldn't use addresses to surmise one's financial status. Behind many a BMW there's a lease agreement the driver can't afford, and behind every address on a well-heeled street was a back office at half the rent.

Bill Langford was a lithe, well-groomed man in his forties. He sported aggressive eyewear, a big-faced watch that looked expensive, and a striped shirt with monogrammed cuffs. He buzzed around the office with a nervous energy and took two telephone calls before turning his attention back to me.

"Sorry about that. Saturday's my busy day," he told me, but he didn't sound at all remorseful.

"It's amazing how we find a way to get it all done," I commiserated. I had learned in an offsite training program that establishing a hierarchy, or eliminating one, was critical in all personal interactions. By using the pronoun "we" I was putting us on equal ground. And to prove that my time was just as important as his, I added, "I have to run to an appointment across town so this should be quick."

Now that the values of each of our respective times were equal, he stopped fussing with his papers and phone calls and gave me his undivided attention.

"So you wanted to talk about the Deakins Building? There's not much I can tell you. I don't represent the owner on that property."

"You made an offer to purchase it."

"Incorrect," he snapped like a middle-school English teacher. "I represented a buyer who made an offer to purchase it."

"Do you do a lot of deals in that area?"

I seemed to have nicked his pride. "I do all types of deals, in all neighborhoods, at all levels," he answered tersely.

"So what happened to this deal?"

"Nothing happened. It fell through."

"Any reason?"

"The seller backed out."

"Did he give a reason why?"

Langford started to answer but then thought better of it. "Who are you?" he asked. I told him my name. "No, who *are* you? An agent?"

I shook my head.

"A broker?"

"No."

"A lawyer?"

"Nope."

"Then why are you wasting my time asking me all of these questions?"

"Ed Vadaresian, the owner of the building you tried to purchase, went missing six months ago and hasn't been heard from since."

I was purposely blunt to match the tone he was using on me but I didn't expect the kind of reaction I got. Langford sat up in his chair, coiled like he was ready to bolt for the door. His movement was slight but very noticeable. Years of grilling associates taught me to pick up on a few things. I also knew the next thing he said would tell me a lot.

"Okay. But what does that have to do with me?" he asked and I knew he was trying to hide something. It was a common deflection technique the guilty use when pressed.

"Nothing, as far as I can tell. I am working with the family to find out some answers."

"What are you, a detective?"

All these careers he accused me of having sounded better than the one I had. I half-wanted to tell him I was a detective. I had this image of some shadowy, marginal figure helping out those in need, someone who settled things with his fists in a time when that only got you sued. "I'm just a friend helping out the family," I told him instead.

"Oh. Why didn't you say so?" he said and returned to his original posture. He leaned back in his chair and his tone changed. He rattled off all he knew like we were two chums catching up on old times.

Langford brokered the deal for the Deakins sale. It was a strange deal from the start. First, Ed represented himself during the sale but had a limited grasp of even basic commercial real estate contracts.

"I was doing more teaching than negotiating!" he said, laughing. Langford admitted that he was tempted to take advantage of Ed, but the deal they were making was good enough as it was. His buyer made a very strong, very competitive, all-cash offer. "Cash is king right now," he added.

"Yeah, I heard that already. Did Ed say why he backed out?"

"He did not," Langford replied. "Can't say it made a lot of sense. Sure, deals fall through all the time. It's part of the business. But this guy Ed was very motivated. There was no activity on his building and we came in with a good offer."

"Any chance he might have gotten a better offer?"

"Have you seen the building?" I told him I hadn't. "No one wants anything to do with that area."

"But you had someone who was interested," I reminded him.

"Special circumstances."

"What does that mean?"

"I shouldn't discuss the details with you," but he continued to anyway. "An investor. I can't give out their name."

"Privacy concerns," I finished for him.

"That's right."

"So no guesses on why Ed would have backed out of the deal?" I pressed.

"Maybe he just ran out of time," he answered.

I pondered that last comment. All morning I lurched toward the conclusion that Ed, under the great financial burden of underwater properties and foreclosure notices, realized that he had no satisfactory exit and decided to make his own by taking his life. But why would he pull out of a deal that would have given him some respite from his money issues? That part made no sense. Also, Ed didn't fit the type, if there was one, who would turn to suicide as an answer.

"What do you mean by 'ran out of time'?"

Langford stared at me with a coy smile. "How much digging have you done?" he asked in a whisper.

"I just started. And why are we whispering?"

"Think of it this way. What's *this* guy doing with *that* kind of building *way* over there?"

I followed his finger as he pointed at a spot on the desk that I imagine represented Ed, then moved to another spot that was the Deakins Building, then a sweeping gesture that could only be referring to Lincoln Heights.

"I have no idea what you're talking about," I told him.

"He wasn't in on this by himself," he lectured. "Everyone has a business partner."

"Okay…"

"He's Armenian…" he said again like that teacher, this time trying to lead the student to the answer. This student was clueless.

"Spell it out for me, please, Mr. Langford."

"Outsiders don't do a lot of real estate deals with Armenians. They are notoriously hard to work with and the ownership structure is always way too murky. Nothing ever has a clear title. And you never know where the money is coming from. One day you're talking to a sweet man like Mr. Vadaresian and the next minute two bruisers in leather jackets and shaved heads are pounding on your door."

❖ ❖ ❖

"Armenian Power?" I laughed. "Isn't that the name of Glendale's utility company?"

Easy Mike didn't laugh at my joke, but I could tell he appreciated it. We stood in line at a small taco stand on the seedier, east end of Melrose Avenue. The *al pastor* was good here, as evidenced by the dozen or so people milling about. A short vaquero with a pot

belly and a straw hat stood just off Mike's shoulder
like he was ready to dart forward and cut in front of
him. It clearly irritated Mike.

"AP is an Armenian organized crime outfit," he explained, then glanced in the potential line-cutter's direction. "They're big in East Hollywood and Glendale and
starting to spread out into the Valley. So go the Armenians, so follows the AP."

"The Armenians have a mob?"

"It's no joke," he said. "These guys are legit. The big
shots—they call them 'Vors'—are all back in Russia.
They run the operation out of there."

We shuffled forward to the order window, and the
vaquero moved in step with us, maybe even a tad closer.

"Can you believe this guy?" Easy Mike said to me.
"I can feel his breath on my shoulder."

"So what do you make of this story?"

"That broker may not be too off. We ran a story on
Armenian Power a few years back after the FBI broke
up an identity theft ring. They're a pretty nasty group,"
he said, moving forward in line and in tandem with
his new friend. "We tried to make a link between them
and Councilman Abramian. He didn't take it too well.
AP has their hands in a lot of pots. Credit card fraud,
Medicaid fraud, mortgage—"

Easy Mike stopped mid-sentence, whirled around to
face the vaquero, and started unbuttoning his pants.

"Jump on in," he shouted and dropped his pants to
his ankles. "You're standing close enough we might as
well be sharing the same pair of *pantalones*!"

For what seemed like the thousandth time since I
had known him, I found myself muttering the phrase

that eventually would be shortened into a nickname. "Take it easy, Mike."

The vaquero gave a confused stare and took a step backward, along with everyone else in line, and finally gave Easy Mike the space he wanted. He turned back to me.

"So mortgage fraud, insurance fraud, any fraud you want, the AP is in it. There are a lot of angles in Glendale."

Easy Mike was one of the first people I fired at the company. It was a simple decision. He was known for his incredibly inappropriate, incredibly antagonistic remarks. His reputation was so terrible I had even contemplated making a "Red Zone" training video made up entirely of examples from his short career with the firm. The proverbial final straw that led to his termination came during the company holiday party.

We were crowded into an ornate salon at the California Club. One of the original partners of the firm stood up to give his annual year-end speech. Everyone had a style at work, be it the roll-up-your-sleeves type or the straight-shooter kind. This particular partner was the "wise sage." He never took a notepad to meetings; thinkers don't have to write down other people's thoughts. His speeches were delivered as if from an atomizer where words hovered over you and one merely had to walk through this mist of knowledge to absorb its wisdom. That fateful night's speech was all about family.

For the better part of twenty minutes, the partner droned on about the importance of your loved ones in life. He mercifully wrapped up his speech with a quote from Dr. Joyce Brothers. "'When you look at your life, the greatest happinesses are family happinesses,'" the partner told us, at which point Easy Mike felt the need to add, "…and whatever piece of ass you can get on the side!"

He got a few nervous laughs, but that was about it. Poor Mike, with one too many gins in him, had picked the wrong time for a wisecrack. As much as this particular partner was known for his "family values" speeches, he was equally known for diddling any new administrative assistant we placed on his floor. The partner glared at Mike, then he looked at me and without words, he passed down the orders for Mike's execution, corporate style.

I called Easy Mike into my office the following morning. I worked over in my head what I was going to say to him, but in the end, didn't need it. When he arrived, he threw his ID badge on my desk.

"Well, it was a good run while it lasted," he announced. "Any chance of a severance package?"

I sadly shook my head.

"Yeah, didn't think so. Let me sign whatever form you got and I'll get out of here," he said, without even a trace of anger.

I hurried through all the protocols and legal documents. According to best practices, I was to escort him to the elevator and ensure he got on. I sheepishly led him out of the office to the lobby. I couldn't let him go without him knowing how I felt.

"Bad timing, Mike," I said.

"What do you mean?"

"You probably weren't aware but that partner you made the comment to has…let's say, a few extracurricular activities outside of the office."

"I know he does," he said and stepped into the elevator. "Why do you think I said it?"

Easy Mike said things everyone else was thinking but were too afraid to say out loud. He eventually found a job at LA's best-known weekly newspaper, where his insolence was not only tolerated but fostered. He quickly made a name for himself exposing the hypocrisies of many a politician and business leader. And it sounded like AP was one of his favorite targets.

"One of their scams is to get some pigeon to purchase a worthless, distressed property but with the promise that they are going to fix it up, turn it into some huge money generator. They get an appraiser who is in on it to over-inflate the price of the property, then take out a silent second on it. The loan money is supposed to go into improvements but instead it goes into everyone's pockets."

"Except the pigeon who bought the place," I added.

"Right. And he's on the hook for the loans."

I made a note to check the value of the property against the amount taken out in loans. Perhaps Ed had fallen into one of these neat little schemes. It certainly helped explain why he would have purchased the Deakins Building, a property that on the surface had very little value unless someone sold him on a fantasy scenario.

Easy Mike promised to dig up whatever files he had on the AP and send them over to me. As we left the taco stand, he asked me about work.

"It is what it is," I said, not really sure what that meant. I didn't want to get into a discussion on my recent career crisis only to have him throw gasoline on the fire by telling me I had wasted the last twenty-five years of my life working there. Instead, he surprised me by saying, "I sort of miss it."

"I thought you hated the place."

"Yeah, but I miss that corporate Asian trim," he said. "How's Amy Tran doing?"

LOCATION, LOCATION, VIEW

The Deakins Building sat west of the freeway on an industrial block close to the river. It was a two-story brick building built in the early part of the twentieth century as were many of the buildings on the street, recalling a time when Los Angeles still manufactured things. This part of Lincoln Heights was too far from the downtown revival, so what could have been prime space for converted condos or artist lofts were now abandoned buildings with the occasional industrial warehouse.

The building clearly hadn't had a tenant in some time. The windows were boarded up and ragweed sprouted out of the cracks in the concrete. A rusty chain-link fence topped with razor wire discouraged the addicts from making this their home. There was an old For Sale sign tacked to the fence with the contact information for GVK Properties. I took down the number.

Circling the building, I found a spot where someone had managed to pry back a bit of the fence. I squeezed through the tight opening and proceeded up the old loading docks. All of the entrances were either boarded up or barred with heavy padlocks. There was a fire escape that I was able to access after pulling down the ladder with a discarded piece of rebar.

I pulled myself onto the roof and was greeted with a magnificent, 180-degree view of the downtown skyline. From this angle, City Hall and the Eastern Building perfectly framed the towering skyscrapers on Bunker Hill. Perhaps this building had some value after all. In Los Angeles, the famous real estate axiom can easily be modified into "Location, Location, View."

Having no other way to snoop around the building, I headed back to my car. I dipped down to slip through the hole in the fence when I heard a woman's voice.

"What do you think you're doing?" she asked.

Startled, I scraped my back against one of the clipped links in the fence. I looked around but didn't see anyone.

"I asked you a question," the voice said again.

I finally spotted its owner sitting in a parked sedan across the street. When we made eye contact, she got out of her car and walked over toward me. She kept her eyes on me the entire time even while crossing the street. She was dressed "corporate casual," which felt out of place on a Saturday in this industrial section of town.

I tried to stand up but my shirt got caught on the fence and I couldn't extricate myself. The more I tried, the more entangled I got. I finally gave up and answered the woman while still hunched over in the fence.

"I was checking out the view," I told her.

"Who said you could do that?"

"Well, no one," I started to explain, then realized there

was no reason to answer her questions. I assumed an air of authority: "I'm not sure that is any of your concern."

"Oh really?" She smiled. It was a nice smile. Then it turned ugly. "Stand up. Turn around. Grab the fence and spread your legs," she barked.

"Huh?"

She pulled back her coat and flashed both a detective's shield and the gun that went with it.

"Now!" she hissed.

"I can't," I admitted. "I'm stuck."

She eyed me suspiciously.

"I'm not lying," I said and showed her where my shirt was hung up on the fence. She contemplated the situation then moved toward me to help. "If you maybe slip it back off the—"

She didn't slip anything. I heard the loud tear of my shirt being yanked from the fence.

"Now stand up and face the fence."

"That's my favorite polo," I muttered pathetically.

"Maybe you should have remembered that before trespassing on private property," she said and removed my wallet. I could hear her pull my driver's license out of its pocket. "Okay, Mr. Restic…" her voice drifted off. "Wait, are you the guy who's been calling me all weekend?"

It took me a while before I figured out what she was talking about. Then I remembered the card Ed's father had given me, and the woman's voice on the message when I called the detective in charge of his case. "I guess you're Detective Alvarado," I said.

"And you're acting very suspicious, Mr. Restic."

"Listen, the family asked me to follow up on his case and to see if you've made any progress. That's why I called you."

She didn't look like she enjoyed being reminded of her lack of success on the case.

"Are you a private detective?"

It was the second time today I was asked that and the second time I regretted having to answer in the negative.

"But the family asked you to get involved?"

"Correct."

"Are you their lawyer?"

Now I was getting annoyed.

"No," I said.

Detective Alvarado didn't know what to make of me, and I couldn't really blame her. She decided to call the Vadaresians and check up on my story. She was able to get Ed's son on the phone and explained the situation to him. As she listened to his response, her eyebrows arched.

"So you're saying you've never heard of this man?"

"That little punk," I whispered under my breath.

"And you never asked for his help?" That cute smile came back to her lips. "Okay, well thank you for your time," she said and hung up the phone.

"He's lying," I said, but it fell on deaf ears.

"Maybe we should drive back to the station and talk this over."

"Am I under arrest?"

"You could be if I wanted to."

"The old man asked for my help. I called you and got your voicemail. Maybe I should have left it there but I got curious and did a little digging—"

"—and trespassing—"

"—and found out some interesting stuff that could help with the case."

"Then we'll have a lot to talk about," she said.

We drove to Glendale in our separate cars after Detective Alvarado had taken my wallet and warned me not to be a hero. On the way I called my wife, Claire. This whole thing seemed innocent enough but one never can be sure. Claire didn't do criminal law but she would know enough to help me out. Maybe I also wanted an excuse to see her. I got her voicemail and left a rambling message.

The Glendale police station was a contemporary glass and steel structure that demonstrated that no expense had been spared when spending taxpayers' money. Detective Alvarado led me through the lobby as various uniformed men eyed us. It felt oddly satisfying to imagine them thinking I was some mastermind criminal being led into his first of many interrogations. Of course, they may have just been ogling Detective Alvarado in her grey pantsuit.

I was led into a small interview room. There was no two-way mirror as I had hoped but there was a closed-circuit camera suspended from the corner of the ceiling. As we sat down I immediately launched into my defense.

"That kid is lying," I told her.

"I know he is," she said to my surprise.

"If you know that about the kid then why am I here?"

"You said you have information, so let's hear it."

"Okay," I said, and launched into a recap of the last two days. I told her about Ed's properties and dire financial situation. I broke the confidentiality agreement and detailed Ed's compensation over the last five years. I also brought up my suspicion that he might be involved with

Armenian Power and relayed Easy Mike's idea that this could have been some sort of mortgage-fraud scheme. She listened intently and nodded a few times.

"Is that helpful?" I asked when I had finished.

"Not at all," she answered quickly. She must have picked up on my disappointment because she added, "It's all good information, but it's nothing I didn't already know."

"So you agree there might be foul play with the Armenian mob? That they may have done something to Ed?"

"No, I never said that," she corrected. "In isolation, what you told me is accurate. But you are applying a narrative to the details that just doesn't exist. Sure, the AP is working mortgage-fraud scams along with a lot of other scams. I've helped put a dozen of their members away myself for crimes similar to those you are describing. But they didn't have anything to do with Mr. Vadaresian's disappearance."

"How can you be sure?"

"Because there's no evidence to support it."

"What about this shady character I saw hanging out with the son?"

"Half of the men in Glendale can be described like that," she shot back. "It doesn't mean anything."

"And the kid pretending that he doesn't know me?"

"He's a punk. Those were your words."

"Don't you think it's odd that a guy like Ed is buying buildings in that part of town?"

"You can't build cases on things that feel odd," she said. Detective Alvarado hesitated as if contemplating whether to share the information she was about to tell me. "There were other people involved in the purchase of that building," she said, but before I could say something she added, "and it wasn't the Armenian Power."

"Who was it?"

"It was a con job. Someone apparently convinced Mr. Vadaresian that the Deakins Building was an investment opportunity too good to pass up and he fell for it."

"Are you going to make an arrest?"

"On Mr. Vadaresian's case, no. But we know who they are and hope to get them before they can pull a similar stunt."

"This still doesn't explain what happened to Ed."

"Mr. Vadaresian was in serious financial peril as you had described. He had recently lost his wife, he—"

"What are you saying?"

"Given his situation it is probably fair to assume that he copped out and killed himself." She said it so coldly. After a brief pause she added, "I apologize if that was too blunt."

"Why didn't you tell the family this?"

"I did," she answered. "They didn't want to listen."

Apparently Ed's father-in-law got very upset with her. If it was a suicide, he demanded to see a body to prove it.

"What about that?" I asked.

"The body will be discovered eventually."

"How do you know?"

"We found Ed's car parked in a lot up in Angeles Forest," she explained. "We searched the area but didn't come up with anything. It's only a matter of time before a hiker stumbles upon the body. I guess the family didn't tell you about that."

They hadn't, but it was starting to make more sense. A missing person can be a real burden on a family. Not only can the relatives not cash in on the person's estate, they also must bear the costs of the estate lest they lose it to creditors. Until a body is found, or several years pass, after which one can legally claim the person dead, the family must maintain the missing person's life, which can be very expensive. The old man's eagerness to find Ed was starting to make sense.

"His father-in-law is the sole beneficiary," I told her.

"I didn't know that," she said, then felt the need to add, "I'm sorry."

"What for?" I asked.

"I don't know, you seem disappointed."

I was disappointed. The search for Ed was already over and with it went the perfect distraction to occupy my time and mind. I looked up at Detective Alvarado, who was staring at me. She averted her eyes when I held her gaze.

The door flung open, breaking the silence in the room.

"I'm Claire Courtwright, Mr. Restic's lawyer."

"Claire, it's okay."

"Get your things, Chuck. We're leaving."

"I don't have any things," I answered dumbly.

"There's no need for theatrics," Detective Alvarado announced. "Mr. Restic and I were simply talking."

"And while y'all were talking, were his rights ever read to him?" The North Carolina drawl came out when she was angry.

"There was no need to."

"Come on, Chuck," she said and led me by the elbow toward the door.

"Thanks, Detective," I said on my way out.

"Sure," she replied with a wry smile.

I thought of something and stopped at the door.

"Detective, if you don't mind me asking, why were you in that neighborhood today?"

"What do you mean?"

"It's far from your jurisdiction in Glendale, and you yourself said Ed's case was all but shut. So why were you hanging out in front of the Deakins Building?"

She laughed.

"You'd make a good detective, Mr. Restic."

"Thanks," I said. "You didn't answer the question."

"I was interviewing someone for another case and saw you skulking around the building, so I stopped to see what you were up to."

"It has a great view," I said.

I apologized to Detective Alvarado for wasting her time and followed Claire out to the parking lot.

"Thanks for coming," I said. "I guess I overreacted a little bit in calling you."

Claire brushed off my apology as she headed for her car.

"I'm not sure I want to know the details."

"Hey, do you have to run?"

"I have to get back to a meeting."

"On a Saturday?"

"Yes. And I've already lost time driving out here."

We hadn't seen each other in weeks and here was Claire buzzing around as if the desire to avoid the topic of our crumbling marriage was propelling her into a sort of perpetual motion. I just wanted to slow everything down.

"Claire, I'm asking for five minutes."

"You're going to the function tomorrow, right? We can talk then." And like that, she flitted away without waiting for my reply.

ELYSIAN FIELDS

"Charity is entertainment for rich people," Easy Mike liked to say.

For five years I'd been on the board of El Sueño, a nonprofit that gave scholarships to college-bound Latinos. It was a worthy cause and an extremely rewarding experience. It provided a wonderful boost to my self-esteem as only the selfless donation of time to a noble cause can do. It was also a terrific résumé builder and a great venue to expand my circle of acquaintances. And the charity auctions at the museum and fundraising galas, like the one I was going to now, rivaled anything the entertainment industry put on, especially if a celebrity chef could be guilted into donating the appetizers. Somewhere down the list, after all the champagne distributors and flower vendors were paid, a handful of deserving students were cut checks to help pay for their books.

The success of a charity was often measured by the status of the people attached to it. I was a small fish when compared to the heavy hitters I rubbed

elbows with. Of course, there was no bigger fish than
Carl Valenti.

Valenti had attained a status in life at which he was
widely known by just his last name. He made his fortune on land developments in Orange County, where
he incorporated cities out of citrus groves and dug
planned communities into the hillsides above them.
At one time he owned nearly three-quarters of the city
of Irvine and was the founding member of the Southland's Eleven-Figure Club. Valenti had recently gained
notoriety in Los Angeles for taking the Anytown USA
feel of his suburban developments and translating it
into "concept," or themed shopping malls. His original
mall, the Elysian, was the site of the charity event.

The Elysian sold nostalgia. Its architectural mélange
of Cape Cod cottage, Georgian revival, Brooklyn brown-
stone, and Southern gothic was so inclusive that anyone
who strolled through its lanes would inevitably recall
some pleasant memory from their past and be overcome with a quiet yearning for home. I made my way
through the main street, where an endless loop of jazz
pumped from hidden speakers, as if everyone's internal soundtracks were set to the cool rhythms of an Ella
and Louis duet. Behind me a conductor cheerfully rang
a brass bell to alert me that his replica streetcar was
slowly approaching.

Everyone at the Elysian seemed to feel a sense of
belonging. No one seemed to notice or care that the
entire thing was an illusion: that the shutters shuttered
blank walls; the wrought-iron balconies led to empty
rooms, and the strings of garland overhead were made
of plastic but sprayed with a chemical to make them

smell like pine needles.

I presented my invitation at the entrance and was led into a giant tent that sparkled with champagne flutes and the bubbly notes of a live pianist. I looked around but didn't see Claire and quietly cursed her under my breath.

Claire specialized in contract work for large commercial real estate firms. The past few years it had meant long hours in the office and longer hours schmoozing at events. The focus on a career was relatively new to Claire. What was once just a way to sound interesting at parties grew into something much more central to her life. While my career hit its zenith years ago with the invention of the Stoplight System, hers was just being born. My slow descent into apathy was paralleled by her enthusiastic rise to partner. Statisticians would say our career paths were inversely correlated.

It quickly became a source of tension between us.

Claire's firm did a lot of the contract work for Valenti's development arm, and as a partner, she had to nurture that relationship. I hadn't realized it also involved nominating me for secretary of one of his hundreds of charities and sentencing me to two-hour board meetings every quarter. Apparently, I wasn't the only one miffed at altruistic conscription.

"If *he* doesn't deem it necessary to be present, why the hell am I here?" I overheard City Councilman Abramian grumble to his chief of staff.

The councilman and Valenti had an on-again, off-again relationship that rose and fell with Valenti's new building projects and Abramian's reelection campaigns. Abramian was very influential in zoning and development issues in Los Angeles. Almost all projects came through his desk, integrally linking him and Valenti. They took turns holding each other over a barrel, but in the end they always found a compromise in which both parties came out on top.

I ran into Bill Langford, the monogram-cuffed broker whose buyer had tried to acquire the Deakins Building, at the cheese table. He was surprised to see me.

"Are you involved with El Sueño?" he asked with a mouthful of smoked gouda.

"I'm secretary of the board."

"Is that right?" he said, looking past my shoulder for the next person he could talk to. These events were for maximizing your connections, and I clearly didn't rate on his list. I didn't want to let him off so easily.

"So I followed up on that building you tried to purchase from Mr. Vadaresian. You were right."

"Right about what?"

"A connection to the Armenian mob."

"Is that so?" he answered in a disinterested fashion, still trying to move on to someone bigger and better.

I went into long, laborious detail of what I had found out and of my conversations with Detective Alvarado.

"Sure, I know Detective Alvarado," he said, trying to hurry me along.

"You do? I don't remember her mentioning you when we spoke."

"Oh. Well, I knew her years ago."

He then spotted someone and excused himself. Unfortunately for him the person he knew was my wife. Claire kissed him hello and immediately brought him back over to me to introduce us.

"Do you know my husband, Chuck? He's secretary of the charity," she said, trying to pass him off on me like a fisherman throwing back the trout that doesn't meet the minimum size requirement.

"Yeah," Langford bemoaned, "he was just telling me."

"How do you guys know each other?" I asked.

"We've done business together," she said, and left it at that just as the speeches were beginning. Langford took advantage of the pause in conversation to drift away.

Councilman Abramian stepped up to the podium and made a generic speech about the importance of the charity and dedication of all the people involved. There was a bit about the future of America and tomorrow's leaders. It was a textbook stump speech—full of praise and entirely devoid of sincerity.

He then gave way to Carmen Hernandez, a local activist and, according to Easy Mike, one of the great shakedown artists of the twenty-first century. She read aloud a poem by one of last year's scholarship recipients. Carmen stole her presentation style from Maya Angelou—over-enunciating random words and punctuating powerful phrases with dramatic pauses that were at least three seconds too long. Even the poem's author squirmed. But the room was rapt with attention. They were, after all, paying for it.

Upon conclusion of the recital, Carmen invoked us to do our part and continue donating to provide a way out for young adults in need. She and Councilman Abramian beat it out of there as soon as their speeches were over. I should have followed them.

I tried to talk to Claire but she spent most of the night flitting around the tent, ducking into pockets of conversations long enough to get in a laugh but short enough to avoid any kind of meaningful discussions. The one pocket she consistently avoided was whichever one I happened to be in. I also noticed another pattern. Claire tended to find herself in the groups that contained a certain square-jawed, blue-eyed man who looked like he rowed crew at Princeton. Even his name—Todd Mc-Intyre—fit the profile. He was Valenti's operations man and dynamo behind the concept malls. He was also someone I suspected Claire had secretly had a crush on for years. The way she laughed at his jokes you would think she was at a Friars Club roast.

Claire was certainly making something of herself. She was mingling with some of the city's power brokers and she loved every minute of it. I realized late into our marriage that that had been her goal all along and the reason she moved west. Los Angeles's secret sauce is that it allows people to be someone they couldn't be back home. It's a place where one can create the kind of large personality and oversize ego that's unsustainable when surrounded by people who actually knew you and would call bullshit.

Claire grew up outside the Beltway with a K Street lawyer father and socialite mother, both functioning alcoholics and incredibly charming. Visiting their home was always entertaining, but it also filled me with a general feeling of inadequacy. Everything was perfect in that household, from the martini with the right amount of vermouth—none—to the level of discourse around the dining room table. They were the kind of people who would actually gather around the piano after dinner to sing show tunes. I'd stand off to the side and smile, nodding my head as I tried to hide the fact that I didn't know the words to the songs. I realized I wasn't alone.

Claire hated visiting her parents and would retreat into a sullen silence on those required holiday trips back east. It was a distinct contrast to the woman I knew and was immediately drawn to—that stylish girl, always talking, always laughing, and exuding a contagious level of confidence. But a lot of it was just a shell that quickly became apparent as soon as we set foot into her childhood home. In that house, there wasn't enough room for three people on the stage. Claire had two choices—sulk in the corner or move somewhere else where she could do the one-act monologue and not have her lines stolen.

It was hard to pinpoint when things started to go south between us, but one day I simply didn't feel comfortable in our house, and that was the first sign that we were in trouble. Not having kids was our biggest mistake. At a certain age, when the careers are on track and the parties and weekend getaways lose their spark, you find yourself looking for something to drive you.

"Transfer all your hopes and failures onto your kids to fulfill," was how Easy Mike put it.

Our relationship felt hollow without the sacrifice of children. We filled our time at farmers' markets and pickling parties and newly discovered restaurants with other childless people, namely Claire's gay friends. On the surface all was going swimmingly well—we were still that fun husband-and-wife team—but under our feet the floor felt squishy, like we were standing on joists in the early stages of dry rot.

But with all our troubles and with every sign pointing to the obvious conclusion that there was no recovering what we once had, I still refused to believe it was over.

Then I saw Claire and McIntyre sucking face in the parking lot like two teenagers on prom night.

I ducked down behind a parked car so they wouldn't see me. *Why am I the one hiding?* I thought to myself, but still didn't get up from behind the car. I heard footsteps approaching and broke into a panic that I would be discovered. It turned out to be Langford again. This time, however, he didn't run from me like the plague.

"Hey, um, I shouldn't have told you that stuff," he said. Langford lacked the swagger from earlier. He looked nervous and distracted, enough to not fully realize he was speaking to a man crouched on the dirty concrete in a parking garage.

"What stuff?"

"About the Deakins Building and that Ed guy."

"You didn't say anything inappropriate."

"I shouldn't betray my clients' trust like that."

"But he wasn't your client," I reminded him.

"All the same, it's not professional."

He lingered like there was more to tell. The longer he stalled, the less he resembled the rainmaking broker. He simply looked like a do-nothing man in an expensive suit.

"Does this have to do with Armenian Power?"

He stared at me for what seemed like an eternity.

"We should talk," I said.

"Okay," he agreed. "But I can't now."

I gave him my card with my cell number jotted on the back. I told him to call me so we could meet. He hurried off.

I called after him to ask if the coast was clear but he was too distracted to hear me.

HE'S GONE

Sometimes people in an emotional free fall precipitate their descent to the bottom so as to shorten the time it takes to return back to the surface. My feet touched bottom in Lincoln Heights.

Lincoln Heights was one of the first beachheads taken in the century-long campaign of suburban sprawl out of downtown Los Angeles. The original developers helped establish a formula that still works today: buy cheap farmland; get someone else (the government) to help pay for the trains and roads to get people to your land; sell the false promise of an Eden in the urban jungle; make a fortune.

The reign of this idyllic middle-class neighborhood, however, was short-lived. The relentless push to replicate the success of Lincoln Heights in other parts drew people farther out to the fringes of the city. Newly arrived immigrants filled the void, and one of the original suburbs of Los Angeles quickly became "undesirable." The coup de grâce was an interstate freeway gashing through the heart of the neighborhood, splitting it in two. Once a destination, Lincoln Heights was now just a route to get you to that next hilltop that overlooks the chaos you're escaping.

When Claire and I separated, I moved out of our Beachwood Canyon home and rented the bottom half of an old Victorian on a street close to the center of Lincoln Heights. Time had chipped away at the gingerbread trimmings, and the house was now a dusty box with bars on the windows and nothing to remind you of its former splendor. The only proof of a past, more grandiose life was the placard on the cornerstone that designated it a historic building. Most of Lincoln Heights sat in a Historic Preservation Overlay Zone, but what they were trying to preserve wasn't entirely clear.

Although I had the means and certainly the time to furnish the place, I never got around to it. I had one chair, a cheap coffee table, a lamp, and nothing on the walls. The bedroom set comprised a mattress on the floor and a stack of books on which sat a reading light. The night after the event at the Elysian, I lay on my bed and stared at the ceiling while thinking about Claire and the incident in the garage, and how faint our whole marriage felt, like someone reminiscing about a long-ago wedding. What was something between the two of us now had a third participant, and the question of how long this person had been involved overran my thoughts. I tried to chase it away, but it was difficult in the silence. It wouldn't be quiet for long. Almost on cue, the music started.

During the day Lincoln Heights was assaulted with the accordion sounds of *norteño* music or the violent ballads of *narco-corridos*, but at night it was all about the doo-wop. In what seemed like a daily ritual, an unseen neighbor would break the relative quiet of the street by playing one of the old, sad songs with their lyrics of longing and lost love. Tonight's song was by the Chantels and had a heartbroken woman plaintively praying to win someone's love back. It was slow and very loud, as if the speaker was sitting on the sill in my bedroom. When the song ended there was a long, silent pause. I heard a woman giggle somewhere outside my window. Then my neighbor did what he did every night— he played the same song over again. His cruelty knew no bounds.

I barely heard the buzzing over the music. I grabbed my pants and pulled out my phone. Not recognizing the number, I debated letting it go to voicemail but decided instead to answer as I didn't have much else to do.

"Mr. Restic?"

"This is he," I said, ever the grammarian at midnight.

"This is Detective Ricohr with the Los Angeles Police Department," he said and paused to let that sink in. "Would you mind coming down to talk with us?"

Cops had a way of making you feel guilty for things you didn't do.

"Sure, what about?" I stammered.

"We'd just like to ask you some questions."

"About?"

"About Bill Langford. He's been murdered."

It was a long-held belief that a direct correlation existed between the value of a neighborhood's property and the police response time to a crime. Apparently, there was also a strong correlation to how quickly they remove a body, because by the time I arrived there was very little evidence that a crime had taken place except for the little yellow cones and a couple of police cruisers. All of the activity was behind Langford's office in a narrow alley with barely enough room to park a compact car. Langford had managed to squeeze his Lexus SUV into the tiny space. The driver door was open and the window was shattered. I hovered behind the yellow tape with a few other gawkers. They were a chatty bunch, and in the short time I was there they'd figured out the entire thing.

"You don't mess with them," a scrawny kid with a voice that rattled fillings explained. "You know what I'm saying? You don't mess with them," he felt the need to repeat. The murmuring around him compelled him to continue. "You know how it is when you mess with professionals. There's no talk." He laughed. "There's just action. That's how they do it. Pop-pop," he demonstrated, which drew a sermon-like agreement from his congregation.

I called the detective's cell phone but he didn't pick up. There were no uniformed officers near where we were standing, so I couldn't alert them that I was there. And I certainly wasn't going to dip under the yellow tape and find them.

"You see how they got him as he came out of the car?" the dishwasher-cum-forensics expert explained. "They was waiting for him. They knew he'd come this way so they was sitting there waiting for him. He pulls in and they come right up behind him—POW!"

"Where were you when it happened?" I asked in as official a voice as I could muster.

"Huh?" he mumbled.

I repeated the question, enunciating each syllable because it sounded like how cops spoke. Everyone in the group stared at me. They weren't quite sure what to make of the stranger interrupting the mini-sermon. The minister was particularly perplexed.

"Why you want to know?" he shot back.

I stared him down.

"I was working," he said without further prompting.

I nodded like I was processing the information.

"You a cop?" someone asked.

I didn't answer but I didn't have to. I looked the group over like I was giving them a warning. Out of the corner of my eye, I saw a uniformed officer approaching and took the opportunity to leave the group hanging, questions unanswered.

"Officer," I called out. "I'm here to see Detective—"

He blew by me without even a look in my direction. The group around me processed what just happened, then burst out laughing. They created such a ruckus that the officer had to come back and quiet them down.

"Keep it down," he warned, "or I am going to send you all home."

It took more than ten minutes of explaining, interruptions from the group, a few calls to other officers, and just plain standing around before I finally convinced him that I was asked to be there and not part of the rabble behind the tape.

"All right, let's go," he said, sounding annoyed. It was a cop's job to always be annoyed.

I shot my new friends an "I told you so" look as the

officer held up the yellow tape so I could pass under it. With his arm raised, I noticed he wore a watch that looked remarkably similar to the one I'd seen on Langford when I had first met him.

Detective Ricohr sat on stairs that led up to the second floor of Langford's building. He was in his mid-fifties and had few distinguishing features. He watched over the proceedings like a bored foreman on an assembly line.

"Larry," he called out to one of the technicians as I approached, "run a GSR test."

A thin Asian man came up with a tackle box and asked me to hold out both of my hands.

"Just a test to see if you've been firing any guns lately," Detective Ricohr answered before I could ask the question.

"Is this legal?" I asked.

"Do you refuse?"

"Can I refuse?"

"Do you want to?"

"Um, sure."

"Smart move," he said and waved away the technician. He patted the spot next to him on the stairs. "Sit down here. I have plantar fasciitis and it hurts for me to stand too long."

"Did you really think I shot this man?"

"We found your card in the deceased's coat. Rather than trek out to wherever the hell you live, it's easier for you to come to us."

"Glad I could help. It's not like I had anything better to do on a Saturday night," I complained, even though I really didn't have anything better to do.

"You'll get over it. How well did you know the deceased?"

"Not well. I've only talked to him a couple of times."

"When was the last time you two spoke?"

"Earlier this evening," I said, though the encounter in the parking lot seemed a long time ago.

"And where was this?"

"At the Elysian. We attended a charity event."

"About what time was that?"

"Sevenish."

The uniformed officer from earlier came over with a plastic evidence bag that looked like it contained a wallet.

"We found this in the dumpster down at the end of the alley," he said, "No money in it."

"Poor guy," Detective Ricohr lamented. "All for a few bucks. Who carries cash anymore?" he asked to no one, even though he waited for an answer. "How much do you have on you?"

"Is this another trick?" I asked.

"Not you," he said. "I was talking to the officer."

"Sir?" the patrolman muttered.

"Maximum, I carry fifty bucks at a time. Plus an emergency fiver in a fold in my wallet in case I get robbed or I blow all my dough on scotch. My mother taught me that trick because the kids used to take my lunch money before I could even get to school. I'd put a quarter in my pocket and two quarters hidden in my shoe. They took the quarter but never knew about the other ones. Stupid kids—lunch was thirty-five cents but they never made the connection. They saw me eat lunch every day but never figured

I had to have more money on me to pay for it," he laughed. "Anyway, leave me that watch before you head back to the station."

The officer stared at him, unsure how to respond.

"Don't embarrass yourself further, son," Detective Ricohr said in a very understanding voice and held out his hand. The officer quietly slipped off the watch and handed it to his superior. Detective Ricohr held it out like he was an admonishing a sixth grader.

"Smarten up, young man," he said and deposited the watch not in an evidence bag but in his own pocket. The young officer stalked off. "Good detectives have to be good criminals. That kid is too much of a dope to be a good crook. Though he almost sent us looking down the wrong path. Did you notice the deceased's wallet? It's one of them breast pocket types. A guy isn't going to go through all the trouble of rolling over a dead body to get at it and not spend an extra five seconds to get the watch right there in front of him. Especially when watches are so easy to hawk."

"So you don't think it was a robbery."

"I don't know what I think. Tell me about this Deakins Building," he said casually. I shot him a look. "They're still looking for the file but so far there's nothing there. Maybe you could fill me in?"

I told Detective Ricohr about my initial meeting with Langford and the encounter we had at the charity event. He half listened and wrote nothing down. I shared what little information I had on Ed's disappearance as well.

"The Armenians are connected?"

"I don't know," I said. "Langford seemed pretty

nervous when I spoke to him earlier tonight. We were going to talk later but—"

"He winds up dead," he finished for me. "Interesting...sort of."

"Do you want the Vadaresian family's contact info? They might have the original documentation on the building transaction."

"You've been a great help, Mr. Restic," he said, dismissing me. "Thank you for coming out."

Detective Ricohr didn't seem all that interested in what I had to say, but then again, he didn't seem like the type to reveal too much of what he was thinking. He reminded me of my first boss at the company. He was the only person I ever met who used the word "nonplussed" correctly. That's because he was the antithesis of the word. Tell him the building was on fire and he'd casually say, "Well, I guess at some point we should make our way downstairs." Nothing bothered him. It was an approach I worked hard to mimic but could never quite replicate. During his retirement party, I pulled him aside and asked him how he could remain so calm through all the corporate chaos he'd encountered over his long career. He answered in the same breezy way he always did: "It's pretty simple," he told me. "I just didn't care."

The local news vans had descended on the scene and were doing live reports at the entrance to the alley. The scrawny character with the drug-hit theory was pontificating in front of the camera. Even they got bored with him and cut him off mid-sentence.

As I slipped under the yellow police tape I noticed a familiar face approaching. Detective Alvarado, looking

casual in jeans, flashed her shield to the uniformed officer and ducked under the tape. I watched her make her
way down the alley and take the seat on the stairs I had
just vacated.

Perhaps Detective Ricohr cared more than I gave
him credit for.

LOVE WHAT YOU DO

One of the most devastating—and reprehensible—acts against members of Corporate America was committed by the self-help guru who convinced workers that in order to be happy they needed to find a job they loved. In a single stroke, he doomed millions of mid-level cogs to an eternal search for something that didn't exist.

The numbers simply didn't support the guru's panacea. Every company has a core set of roles that is central to what it does as a business. These jobs are the main circuit that gives a company life, and the people in those roles feed off the energy of "feeling a part" of something. But for every role on that circuit, there are twenty more in areas that have nothing directly to do with the company's business—senior account liaisons, meeting and planning specialists, content development coordinators—roles that have a function but little value and ultimately are wholly unsatisfying. The guru makes his fortune from this group as they gobble up iteration after iteration of the same false promise.

The true believers quit their stable, well-paying jobs to open up hand-crafted candle businesses out of their garages. The rest play an endless game of switching careers in the hope of finding that elusive one for which every paycheck brings a big dose of happiness. That search is so common that anytime an associate shows up at work wearing a suit, you naturally assume an interview is scheduled. When the person leaves at midday for a "doctor's appointment," it is common to wish him or her good luck.

The week after my very brief stint as a private detective, I found myself roaming the halls a bit more at work. My daily duties had lost some luster from their already fairly lusterless base. On one of my rounds, I noticed someone emerge from one of my legacies at the company—the Resting Room. Expecting a woman in her second trimester, I instead saw a young man carrying a portfolio. He saw me and sheepishly slunk back to his cubicle. Everyone knows to fear HR. The poor guy hadn't remembered to tuck his résumé back into its folder. So he was using the room for a phone interview, highlighting the challenge of legions of cubicle dwellers—how to actively job search when your supervisor can hear everything you say and see everything on your screen. It comforted me that the Resting Room provided such a valuable service—unintended, sure, but still valuable.

Then I remembered Ed and his admission when I confronted him about his cologne. He thought I was reprimanding him for using the phone in the Resting Room. This piqued my curiosity. Working backward on the dates, it appeared that Ed disappeared on the day I had spoken to him. And perhaps those calls he made would provide some clues about what happened to him. After all, if they were "I'll pick up bread on the way home" calls, he would have placed them from his cubicle. But to search out privacy, like our young interviewee had, spoke to something larger.

I pulled the phone records on the days leading up to Ed's disappearance. It took a little maneuvering to get this information because of privacy concerns, but I used the young interviewer I discovered misusing the room as an excuse to dig deeper into other potential issues. The list of phone calls was surprisingly long. I settled in at my desk with a big cup of coffee and started making my way through the list.

The calls could be broken down into two main groups: the Job Seekers and the Personal Crises. The first group was your typical set of corporate recruiters, resume builders, life coaches, and HR folks at other firms. The Personal Crises group laid out neatly on a seriousness scale starting with the minor (Quit Smoking Hotline), elevating to the grave (Planned Parenthood clinics), edging into the critical (Free STD Testing), and culminating with the dire (a phone-sex line with lactating women). I imagined the heightened sense of pleasure this particularly disturbed individual must have gotten from placing the call from a room dedicated to mothers.

Once I eliminated those two groups, it was easy to isolate which calls Ed had placed. The day before he went missing, there was a call made to Emerald Properties, undoubtedly to Langford, who was working on the deal for the Deakins Building. Within minutes of making that call, two more were made in succession. There was a lapse of about five minutes and then a final call. After that there was a three-hour interval before the next call was placed. I assumed that the first two calls and possibly the third were all made by Ed.

The first number led to a surprising location—the Glendale Police Department. It was the number to the main switchboard, so there was no way to tell with whom he spoke at the station. The call lasted only a minute and so it was likely he never made it out of the automated recordings. It made me wonder if Ed knew he was in some sort of danger and sought help from the police.

I dialed the next number on the list, and a heavy, accented voice mumbled something incomprehensible when he answered. There was a lot of indistinguishable noise in the background. It sounded more like a business than residence.

"Hello?" I said hoping he would repeat what he said when he answered the phone.

"Yeah," he said instead.

"Who's this?"

"Huh?"

"With whom am I speaking?" I said full of formality.

"What happen?" a confused voice replied.

"What's your address?"

"Oh," he answered, and his voice brightened at his finally being able to understand what I was saying. He rattled off an address to somewhere in south Glendale on San Fernando Boulevard.

The third and final number led to a voice recording for Signature Homes. According to the pitch, they

offered an oasis of comfort living in an urban landscape.
I finally got a live voice on the line and immediately
wanted to return to the recording.

"How might I make your dreams of home ownership come true?" she offered. When confronted with
these types of personalities, my instinct is to turn sour.

"I live in Lincoln Heights with my mother," I blurted out.

"We have a number of options to fit any lifestyle,"
she replied so quickly that I wondered if she'd even listened to what I had said. "So are you and your mother
looking together?" Apparently, she had.

"I have bad credit."

"You'll be surprised at the range of loan-servicing
options available to you."

"I'm recently unemployed," I tried again.

"We can always work something out where your
mother would be the primary borrower," she said. "Why
don't we set up a time to walk through some wonderful
opportunities?"

A stint at the Guantanamo detention center couldn't
break through her relentless cheerfulness. I made an appointment with a phony name and Claire's cell phone
number and hung up. I took stock of my one lead, the
address in Glendale, conjured up a doctor's appointment, and headed out.

My co-manager Paul caught me in the elevator lobby
with my laptop bag. As I stepped onto the elevator, he
wished me luck.

San Fernando Boulevard winds like an asphalt river
through the industrial areas of Glendale, with its

unmarked warehouses and occasional low-end strip joint. The address led me to a dingy tire-repair shop where every surface looked like it had been smeared in charcoal. As I approached, the proprietor glanced at the tires on my car as a barber would eye the hair on your neck.

"How much to fix a slow leak?" I asked.

He gave me the once-over, twice, then quoted a price that was at least five times the normal one. And people claim discrimination only targets minorities. My tolerance for the "white-guy price" was at its limit.

"Great!" I said and pointed out the culprit. As he worked on the tire, I probed him for information. "A friend of mine recommended this place—Bedros Vadaresian." I watched for a reaction and got none. "Do you know Ed?"

He leaned on a steel rod and walked like a mule around the hand-cranked wheel mount, pausing briefly to dip his hand in a pool of gray water, which he rubbed on the tire to check for leaks.

"There's no leak here," he said accusingly.

"Oh really? I've been having to fill it up—"

The office door opened and five Armenian men poured out. None of them worked there, as evidenced by their spotless clothing. One of the men stopped to get a better look at me.

"I know you," he said. Of course he knew me. He was the man I'd seen with Ed's son on the front porch to his home. "What are you doing here?"

Before I could continue with my story, the mule with the steel rod rattled off something in Armenian. The only words I picked out were Ed's name. The other men grew interested and formed a half circle behind me.

"Fellas," I said, which sounded like an invitation for a beating. "I don't know what's going on."

"What you want with Ed?" the mule asked me, yanking the steel rod out of the wheel mount. It clattered and scraped on the concrete.

"Nothing." I started out well but my composure soon devolved into blabbering. "The family asked... you know...I'm just...with the tire here...and a slow leak...."

I bolted. I ducked between two of the thugs behind me and ran. I ran out of the tire shop, turned north on San Fernando, and never looked back. I had to stop three blocks later because my lungs felt like they were being shredded with razor blades. The pain from running was nothing compared to the shame at having chosen to run in the first place. Twenty years as an HR executive had earned me a black belt in passive aggression, but it had also completely erased any capability in the old-fashioned, violent kind.

I sulked along for a few blocks and tried to blot out the last fifteen minutes. I would have gone home and dropped the whole matter except for a small detail—my car was still back at the garage. I decided to check in with Detective Alvarado, leaving out, of course, the part about running away. She was at the precinct so I took a bus up to the station.

"Are you okay?" she asked.

"Yeah, why?"

"You don't look so good."

I told her about the discoveries I made from the Resting Room phone records and my run-in at the tire shop.

"They assaulted you?" she said and sprung to her feet, ready to confront the assailants.

"Well, I wouldn't choose that word," I said, trying to temper her a bit.

"Which word would you choose? Did they threaten you?"

"Verbally?"

"I can't think of any other way, unless they wrote it out on an index card."

"It was a threatening environment, but I wouldn't go so far as to say they threatened me."

She was amused by the parsing of words. "I don't think we could make environmental threatening stick. You're sure about the man being the same one you saw last week?"

"Positive."

"Then let's see if we can put a name to a face."

I spent the next thirty minutes poring over mug shots. After about a dozen it became one big blur of faces. But then I saw him. His hooked nose stood out. I pointed him out to Detective Alvarado.

"Ardavan Temekian," she read out loud.

"You know him?"

"Somewhat. He's a junior Vor, but he's moving up the ranks."

"I wonder why Ed called him. It's a pretty big coincidence that he disappeared a day later."

"Enough coincidences strung together stop being coincidences," she said.

"And now Bill Langford getting killed," I added.

She cocked her head to one side.

"When did you hear about that?"

"The other night when I spoke to Detective Ricohr. He called me a few hours after the murder. What did you guys talk about?"

This time she laughed. "You really do get around."

"I saw you coming in as I was leaving. One thing I wanted to ask you," I said. "When I first mentioned talking to Langford, you never mentioned that you knew him. How come?"

"My husband knew him," she started after a long pause. Her voice trembled slightly. "He passed away not too long ago and I guess I am still having trouble getting over it. These reminders of him keep coming back."

"I'm sorry."

"It's probably better for me to get it out."

"Why did the detective want to speak with you, if you don't mind me asking?"

"You are definitely persistent. I shouldn't discuss this with you, but Bill Langford called me before he was killed."

"He did? What did he want?"

"I don't know. He left me a message that we needed to talk. I haven't spoken to him in years. I never did get a hold of him."

Langford had looked pretty shaken when I saw him in the parking lot. Perhaps he'd called in an old acquaintance for help.

"Are you still thinking Ed killed himself?" I asked.

"I'm much less convinced than I was yesterday," she answered.

Detective Alvarado walked me out of the police station. She promised to follow up on the call placed to the Glendale station, but she didn't have much hope as the main line wasn't tracked like the one to 911. She kind of hovered like she didn't want to part just yet.

"I don't know your situation," she began, "but maybe one of these days we could go grab a drink?" For the first time since I met her, the controlled Detective Alvarado suddenly looked vulnerable.

"I'm married," I blurted out.

"Oh," she blushed. "I didn't know that."

"But we're separated."

"Okay."

"So I'd be up for that drink."

She smiled, but I could tell she was regretting the decision to ask me out. If the conversation was a fraction as awkward as the last thirty seconds, she knew she'd be in for a long night. As I walked off, I realized I didn't know how to pronounce her first name.

"Ar-ree-sell-ee," she said. "But just call me Cheli."

I took the bus back to the tire shop. It was well after six, and the shop was shut tight. My car had been courteously pulled out onto the street, with the added benefit of a deep gash in all four tires.

CLOCK RUNS OUT

There was a moving truck in front of Ed's house. A couple of day laborers hefted a couch onto the front lawn and left it there in the hot sun. They were equally careless with the other pieces of furniture. Neighbors watched through slits in their curtained windows. That would be the second time they had done it—the first when the family moved in and they were too shy to introduce themselves, and now, as the family moved out and they were too embarrassed to face people who had lost their house to foreclosure.

I scanned the yard but didn't see Ed's son or father-in-law. As I got out of my car to go investigate, I heard a voice call out behind me. Ed's son sat on the hood of his car on the opposite side of the street. He watched over the proceedings like a detached observer.

"What happened?"

"What do you think happened?" Rafi said bitterly. "The bank took the house. It's my father's last gift to the family."

"I'm sorry, Rafi."

"What are you doing out here?"

"I want to give your grandfather an update on your father's case. I've been speaking with the detective in charge and although they don't have any good news, there have been some developments. Is he around?"

"Papik?" he said, laughing. "No, he took off."

"What do you mean?"

"He grabbed his stuff the other night and left me with this mess to deal with."

"Do you know where he went?" I asked.

"He's probably staying with my uncle out in the Valley. In Van Nuys or somewhere."

"Where are you going to stay?"

"Not there," he said. "They don't have any room. Plus, I doubt they want to see my face. It'll remind them of all the money my father owes them."

So the relatives served as a source for the seed money in Ed's real estate deals. I didn't blame him for wanting to steer clear of that group—there's nothing worse than the glare from someone you owe money to.

"Relax," he said, anticipating my question, "I'm going to crash at a friend's here in Glendale."

He leaned back against the windshield and surveyed the scene. More than once there was movement behind the various curtains, shutters, and blinds as his eyes passed over his neighbors' homes.

"They're all afraid this is going to happen to them," he said with a wry smile. No longer was Rafi the detached observer. He was a willing participant in a housing game he never knew he was playing. Where his grandfather slipped out in the middle of the night, Rafi put himself on display in the hot sun until the very end.

"Why did you lie about talking to your father when I first came out here?" I asked him.

"Who said I lied?" he shot back but the fight wasn't in him.

"You never spoke to him," I stated more as a fact than a question. Rafi simply shook his head. "Were you just being a punk or was there a reason?"

He suddenly remembered another lie he had made.

"Whatever happened with that detective that called asking about you?"

"The one you told you never knew me?"

"Yeah."

"She put me under arrest," I said.

"Because of me?" he laughed.

"I don't find it funny," I said, pretending to be angry.

"I do."

I let him enjoy the moment. It wasn't that he found the episode all that amusing, but it was a way to thumb his nose at all the prying neighbors. Maybe he did lose his house, but at least he could laugh about it.

"My friend wanted me to say that stuff about talking to my dad," he offered up.

"Why?"

He shrugged it off.

"How do you know this Temekian character?"

"How do *you* know him?" he asked.

"I know he's a crook."

"Ain't we all."

"Aren't we all what?"

"I'm Armenian, man," he shrugged, trying to make light of my question.

"I don't find that funny," I said for the second time,

although in this instance, I didn't have to pretend to be angry. "Temekian is in the mob and not a person you should be associating with. He's involved in some pretty rough stuff, Rafi. You're better than that."

"Who the hell are you? This guy does all right as far as I can see."

"I'm telling you what I know," I said, aware that I was starting to lecture. "There are better ways to make something of yourself."

"I don't see anyone taking his house," he said. The resentment toward his father was going to take a long time to get over. "He's helping me."

"With what?"

"With money."

I didn't answer and let him fill in the blanks.

"We can sell some property before the bank takes it," he explained.

"Which property? The Deakins Building?"

He nodded.

The poor kid was being taken for a ride. There was no way he was going to make any money off the sale of that building. I then realized why he lied about speaking with his father. You need a live person to conduct a real estate transaction, unless you falsify the documents.

"If you forge any documents, you are the one going to be left holding the bag," I warned. "Trust me on this, Rafi. They are playing you. These guys don't care about you. There's something very fishy going on with that property. Don't get involved and we'll try and work this out."

Rafi pretended not to listen, but I think I was getting through to him. Avoiding Temekian and his associates was a start, but it certainly didn't help the kid out with his current situation. I made a motion for my wallet, but he stopped me.

"I don't need your money," he said and jumped down off the car.

☀ ☀ ☀

GVK occupied the back unit of a mini–strip mall on the northern end of Verdugo. There was no sign to identify the company. It was situated next to a gift store that sold fake crystal figurines and other tchotchkes that were doing a brisk business collecting dust. The strip mall apparently collected rent every month, but where these businesses were getting the money from was a mystery. I had no trouble finding a parking spot.

The office was a narrow space with several desks angled on each side. There were a couple of people inside, but largely the desks were empty. No one greeted me when I entered. In fact, it was like I didn't exist. One man whispered into the phone. Another stared at a piece of paper like he was trying to hypnotize it. At last a third man came out of the back room. He walked right past me toward the exit but turned back, almost like he was surprised someone was standing there. He didn't speak; he just arched his eyebrows, which was my cue to start talking.

"Is there someone I can talk to about a building you represent down on Asher?" I asked.

The man shouted out some name and immediately turned for the door and left.

"How can I help you?" boomed a new voice from the back room. Out came a large, well-dressed man with one of those shirts where the collar and cuffs are a different material than the rest of the shirt. The cuff links were either lapis or plastic. "You had a question about a property?"

"I represent a client who is interested in one of your properties. The Deakins Building in Lincoln Heights."

"Yes, a new listing for us," he said, smiling. "Come, let us get a coffee." He led me outside.

We walked out to the front of the strip mall where a small café catering to middle-aged Armenian men served Turkish-style coffee and brazenly ignored the city's no-smoking laws. The men inside were more fixtures than patrons. How this business subsisted was another mystery. The only activity was the lighting of more cigarettes and the occasional shifting in chairs to stave off developing bedsores.

We used two tables to spread out the myriad documents he brought over on Deakins. The man had told me his name, but it was so long I already had forgotten it. All the Dale Carnegie memorization techniques combined couldn't come up with a trick to remember that one.

The man rattled off a string of details on the Deakins Building including net operating income, cap rates, and a figure on occupancy vouchers. It seemed buildings carried this number as a way for the city to control congestion and high-density issues. As a former manufacturing facility, Deakins carried with it a very large number, which, by the way the man kept talking about it, seemed to be worth something.

"This is a relatively new listing for you?" I asked.

"Less than a year."

"Can you fill me in on its history? I see it sold for quite a hefty price six years ago." Ed had paid top dollar times ten for this building.

"The economy," he lamented, but even the Great Recession couldn't justify the magnitude in price drop I was seeing.

"Even so," I pressed, "the last sale seems a bit out of line with the comps. It's a real outlier."

"Maybe, maybe not," he deflected, then added, "we had high hopes for that building when we first bought it."

"Are you a part owner of the building?"

"Now? No, no, we're not owners."

"But you were?"

"I wouldn't say that," he said. "We were involved in the original sale." Everything was starting to feel incestuous. Sensing my confusion, he added, "We didn't work directly on that deal."

"But you worked indirectly on it?"

"I can't remember. We may have done an assessment of the property." He waved like it was barely worth mentioning. I remembered Easy Mike's point about the role of the assessor on mortgage-fraud schemes. The players were starting to fall into place.

There was a risk the man would shut down if I got too aggressive with my questions. One of the best interviewing techniques I learned was to identify the tone the interviewee was taking and mimic it.

"Oh, okay," I said casually, waving my own hand like he had. "So you weren't really involved in the original deal. You seem like a smart man, and I was just wondering why you'd be involved in a deal like that!"

And he laughed right along with me.

"Remember the times," he explained. "There was a real boom going on and the downtown revitalization was just starting up. The Brewery Artist Lofts had opened and were a huge success. We wanted to mirror that success with the Deakins."

The Brewery project took an old Pabst Blue Ribbon facility in a seedy part of downtown Los Angeles and converted it into lofts and artist studios. Hipsters living on daddy's dime gobbled them up and lived the poor artist's life in million-dollar condos where parking was extra. This scenario was being played out all over downtown. Development money funneled into the three-mile radius. Abandoned buildings were converted into lofts and restaurants and galleries.

If you left out the part about the heroin addicts urinating in front of your building, you could see how someone like Ed could fall for a pitch like this. Lincoln Heights was the next downtown. The Deakins was the next Brewery. There were millions to be made. But the people Ed listened to had no intention of seeing the Deakins turned into the next urban oasis.

"What's the ownership structure?" I asked.

"One owner."

"An individual or a corporation?"

"Individual."

"Is he motivated? I am going to need a smooth transaction and want to avoid any ugliness from the seller's end."

I got a look that warned me to slow down.

"There shouldn't be any problems," he answered simply.

We walked back to his office, and I promised to be

in contact soon. A voice called out to me as I was getting into my car.

"What are you doing here?" Claire asked as she came striding toward us.

"Hello, Arshalouys," she chirped and did the two-kiss greeting. Apparently her name-remembering skills were more honed than mine. "Do you know Chuck?"

I tried to remember if I had given my real name. I hadn't, but Arshalouys didn't seem to notice.

"I never got your card," he said to me. Maybe he did notice.

"Actually, I must have left them at the office."

"Anytime someone uses the word 'actually,' it means they are lying," Claire felt the need to add. "You told me that once, Chuck."

"Yeah. Okay. Anyway, I have to run—"

"Hey Chuck, did you hear about what happened to Bill Langford?"

The mere mention of that name gave Arshalouys whiplash. He glared at me.

"Yeah, tragic."

"Right after we talked to him," she said.

"I don't know about right after," I corrected. I snuck a peak at Arshalouys, whose eyes were locked on me and not letting go.

"You guys were chatting it up. Did he say anything? The *Times* said it was ruled a homicide."

"Just small talk."

"It's crazy," Claire babbled on. "How you can be talking about a cheese plate without a clue that it's the last conversation you'll ever have."

"Well, that's life," I said and jumped into my car. I

was desperate to extricate myself from this conversation. As I pulled out of the lot, I could still feel those eyes boring in on me. It wasn't until I was halfway home that I realized I was so busy trying to deflect Claire's questions, I didn't have time to ask the more important question.

Why was she meeting with this man in the first place?

HEROES

The Los Angeles Police Academy was a rambling complex of about twelve buildings and a shooting range nestled in the hills beneath the giant plateau that is Dodger Stadium. It was more than just a training ground for new recruits. The Academy also had the Revolver and Athletic Club, which included a swimming pool for officer families and a café that was open to the public. I was surprised Easy Mike chose this place to meet for lunch, as he wasn't particularly fond of the police in general and they weren't fond of him. Over the course of three years he had written a series of scathing exposés on corruption and incompetence— two traits that seemed to go hand-in-hand with the Los Angeles Police Department—that earned him NFF status (no friend of the force) among the upper echelons of the force.

We sat in one of the empty Naugahyde booths along the window. Aside from the waitresses and busboys, we were the only two people in the room without guns. We got a few looks when we came in but it was more to see if someone of higher rank was worth kissing up to. Mike and I didn't look like cops, and the room immediately lost interest in us.

"This place gives me the willies," Mike said.

"Then why did we come here?"

"They have a good patty melt."

The waitress brought us menus and waters and innocently asked Mike if he wanted a straw.

"Of course I do," he replied. "You think I want to put my lips on the same glass some pig drank out of?"

More than a few heads turned in our direction.

"Jesus, take it easy, Mike," I whispered and slunk low in the booth.

"I'm just busting balls," he said.

"Why do you have to be so antagonistic?"

"Because these guys walk around with chips on their shoulders and there's no one left to knock them off to keep them honest." Keeping the police in check was a favorite topic of his. "The worst development of the last twenty years," he went on, "is the cozy relationship between the press and the police. This is supposed to be a system of checks and balances. Now the *Times* reads likes a glorified Benevolent Society newsletter extolling the virtues of these everyday heroes."

What Mike never advertised was the fact that his father was one of those "heroes" who was killed on a random evening some twenty years earlier. Mike let the story slip one night under the powerful influence of too many Bushmills at the Anchor Bar on Third Street. Like his writing, the story was lean and filled with a few haunting details.

Mike's father was a detective and twenty-year vet

on the force. He worked out of the Rampart Division and commuted all the way out to Covina, where Mike and his family grew up. On one of those drives home, Mike's father pulled off the 10 Freeway to stop at a convenience store in El Monte and he stumbled onto a teenager beating the clerk senseless with a tire iron. The detective intervened but never saw the accomplice lurking in the aisle. The accomplice, whom they later caught and put to death, casually approached Mike's father and stabbed him six times in the side with a Phillips-head screwdriver he had just stolen from a neighbor's shed. "It was technically seven, but the first attempt didn't puncture so it wasn't counted in the total," he told me that night. Ever the journalist, Mike had tracked down the investigating officers and convinced them to let him read the entire police report. He seemed to find comfort in the details.

"We need to get back to the day when no one liked cops," he explained as the waitress delivered his patty melt. "That way they don't get too comfortable throwing their weight around without consequences."

"You got your Irish up today."

"For good reason," he said and slid over a fat accordion file.

"What's this?"

"A big story." He smiled.

The folder contained copies of countless real estate deals and contracts and spreadsheets. I flipped through them randomly as Mike explained what he had discovered.

"Three buildings were recently purchased as part of a big community redevelopment program by my old friend Carmen Hernandez." She was one of Mike's favorite targets in his column. Under the guise of community activist and Latino community do-gooder, she ran a mini-empire that afforded her a beautiful family compound in Monterey Hills. She was a master manipulator in that hazy area between politics and business. Reciting bad poetry at charity functions was just part of her PR work. "The buildings are going to be converted into a women's center," Mike continued. "It's all a sham. Dedicating a portion of your building to some social cause gets you a development grant from the city. They help buy the building and fund the construction."

"Where's the scam?"

"I said 'portion' of the building. Once it's built, you can do what you want with the rest of it, including charging real rents. Under a 'not-for-profit' status, the city never sees a dime back."

"How do they get away with it?"

"Mostly by having friends in high places. Councilman Abramian holds the purse strings to the redevelopment money in that area. What he says goes. He's up for reelection this fall and must be trying to shore up his base with the Latino vote. As much as I dislike Carmen, she is true to her word. When she gets paid off, she delivers the goods. Now comes the interesting part," he said, leaning forward. "Who do you think brokered all three deals?"

"Langford."

"Who took the big shove last week."

Mike was on his game and he knew it. He had culled the documents and painstakingly created a matrix of all the names, connections, and overlap to create a narrative showing how the various participants were involved. It must have taken countless hours to do it, and it got me thinking about the "love what you do" fallacy. When Mike was in the middle of a story he was excited about, no one saw him for days on end. He was consumed by the work and driven by a manic anger to plow ahead to its conclusion. He would eventually surface looking haggard and a few years older.

The self-help guru would tell Mike that the extreme level of passion he put into his work was because he had found a career that he loved. And the guru couldn't be more wrong. For Mike, it was all about the struggle. He was most alive when embroiled in a scrap, whether it was calling out a pompous executive for his dalliances or exposing crooked parking-enforcement officials for selling handicapped placards. It had nothing to do with some moral code but everything to do with being in a fight.

"This is right next to the Deakins Building, the one Ed owns," I said, pointing to a map of the buildings in question.

"It's getting chummy all of a sudden, isn't it? Does this name ring a bell? Arshalyous Begossian?" Apparently I was the only one who couldn't pronounce his name.

"It should. I just met with him yesterday about Deakins."

"He's been brought up on ethics charges twice but cleared both times. They involved allegations of mortgage fraud. He is also rumored to be in tight with the Armenian Power."

"Claire was meeting with him."

Mike studied me for a moment.

"I was wondering when you were going to tell me that little detail." He tapped the manila folder. "Her name and her law firm pop up in these documents. They were working with Langford on the zoning. I'm not sure of the details but they have their hands dirty."

"What do you mean 'they'?"

"You know what I mean. Claire's firm has only one real client."

"Why would Valenti get involved in this kind of stuff? It's child's play. Seems like a stretch."

"Listen, you got a nose for shiraz, but I got a nose for scumbags. And this one stinks."

"So what are you going to do?"

"What are *you* going to do?" he shot back. "I want you to talk to Claire."

"About what?"

"This! You need to confront her."

I didn't have much fight in me. My marriage was teetering and I didn't want to do anything to tip the scale one way or the other.

"What would I even say to her? So she has worked with people of questionable character. So have you. And so have I, for that matter."

"She's running all over you," he challenged.

"No she's not."

"Who left whom? And don't give me some bullshit about it being mutual. In the history of relationships there hasn't been a single instance of a mutual breakup. Is she sleeping with someone?"

"Mike, it's not about that."

"That's a 'yes.' What's his name?"

"I don't want to talk about it," I said. The last thing I wanted to tell Mike was about McIntyre and Claire. That was only more fuel to his fire.

"She's moved on, pal," he said, taking the antagonistic approach.

"Don't call me *pal*."

"She's moved on, *buddy*," he corrected, which was even more irritating. "And I don't want to see you sit here and take it. You want her back?"

"Sure."

"Then go get her. If not, then ruin her."

"Great advice," I said, getting up from the table to head to the restroom, and far away from this conversation.

"There are no more consequences to actions anymore!" he shouted after me. "Sometimes we have to set things straight ourselves."

I stood at one of the urinals and tried to push down the emotions Mike had stirred up about Claire. I simply wanted all of it to go away. I recalled that first week after the separation. She wanted space, and I got more than anyone would ever want. I spent a few nights in a business hotel downtown that catered to the nearby corporations and their global workforces who breezed through for a three-day stint in the Los Angeles office. Occasionally I ran into a lost German tourist who amazingly found pleasure in the sterile, empty streets of Bunker Hill at night. A friend convinced me to get out of the hotel lounge and spend some time with his family out in the Valley. There are times when someone's generosity is almost enough to restore one's faith in all humanity. My friend upended his family's life by moving his daughter into the top bunk in his younger son's room. I was given an open-ended invite, and he meant it, but I didn't last more than a day. After a home-cooked meal and a cigar on the back deck, I settled into a preteen's purple polka-dotted room. My feet hung over the edge of the twin mattress and I stared at a glow-in-the-dark constellation on the ceiling. And I never felt so lonely in my life.

"Your friend has a big mouth," a voice said behind me.

I finished up at the urinal and turned to face two young officers. They couldn't have been more than a few months from graduation. I could still smell the talcum powder from their haircuts.

"I know he does," I told them and headed for the sink. They fell in step behind me and stood off each shoulder.

"He should know better," the second officer chirped. They didn't seem capable of formulating a compound sentence. I looked at them in the mirror. They were at an age where pride still mattered. And they were quick to defend it.

"He's sitting out there. Go tell him."

That didn't go over too well. Much like Mike, I never was a big fan of the police, and my low opinion must have slipped into the tone of my voice, because I watched both of the young officers bristle and roll up onto the balls of their feet. The one on my left grabbed hold of my shoulder and spun me around.

"Never mind telling us what we should be doing," he said.

"We'll talk to who we want to talk to," the other one finished.

"Guys, I apologize for my friend out there. We don't

want any trouble." I was hoping that was the end of it, but apparently I needed to be subjected to a speech.

"He should learn some respect," one of them began. "We put our lives on the line—"

"—to protect and to serve."

"Do you know what kind of shit we have to put up with on a daily basis?"

"The kind of bullshit we have to do while we're out there making the streets safe for people like you?"

The banter was tired but they did make a great tandem. I was grateful Mike wasn't there to witness this. I had an image of an index finger and a thumb playing the world's smallest violin.

"Where are these mean streets that you speak of?" boomed a mocking voice. A pit formed in my stomach as my initial thought was that Mike had stumbled upon us and was going to turn this encounter into a full-blown incident. But no one had entered the bathroom.

The young officers and I looked around trying to place the voice. Then we heard a newspaper rustle and realized that it came from one of the stalls. I looked to the two officers. One of them was confused and in no mood to investigate. The other wasn't so quick to give up. He approached the stall.

"What'd you say in there?" he asked the door.

"I said, 'Get your uniforms dirty before you start swapping war stories in a public restroom.' "

Just as the officer was about to go tell the voice where he could put his advice, we all heard movement in the stall and then a detective's shield slid out from under the door and settled at the young officer's feet. He looked at his partner and together they saw their fledgling careers stumble before they could get out of the gate. They decided to quietly slip out of the bathroom. I started to follow them out.

"Wait a minute, would you?" the voice beckoned. "I want to talk."

Unfortunately for me, it was longer than a minute. After five page turns I called out, "What are you doing, the crossword?"

"Funny," he grunted and finally emerged from the stall. "They have a great patty melt, but it doesn't always sit well with me."

Detective Ricohr shuffled his feet out of the stall. His pants were still around his ankles. His legs were hairless and a color bordering on translucence. I conjured up a large, imaginary piece of cardboard just below my nose that kept my eyes from seeing what was below.

"Thanks for intervening before," I said, my gaze looking somewhere at the crown of his head.

"You'd have thought those two punks were in the North Hollywood shootout," he said with a laugh. "Still doesn't make up for the nonsense your friend is throwing around out there. He's begging for a beating."

"I feel sorry for the guy who gives it to him."

"Oh yeah? Is he tough?"

"Only in print."

Detective Ricohr went to the sink and washed up. He then proceeded to tuck his collared shirt into the elastic waist of his cotton briefs and pulled the shirttails out the bottom. He caught my look.

"My dad taught me this trick," he smiled. "Keeps the shirt tight on the chest, no creases." And then without missing a beat, "Who's Paul Darbin?"

Naturally, I knew the name, but the context in which I was being asked led me to stare dumbly at Detective Ricohr.

"Paul Darbin?" I repeated, which is a sure sign that you either don't know the answer to the question, or you are stalling to make up an answer.

"Yeah, I think he works with you."

"Oh, Paul, sure I know him. We co-manage a group in Human Resources."

"How long have you known him?"

"Has to be almost fifteen years."

"Fifteen years and it still took you a while to place the name," he stated in an accusatory manner.

"Sorry, the police academy bathroom setting threw me off. I know him from the office."

"Let me go over some names: Ed Vadaresian, Bill Langford, Paul Darbin, Claire Courtwright. All these names are connected and there's one link—you know all of them." He calmly stared in my direction.

"Must be a coincidence," I said but my voice faltered. Cops rivaled Catholic priests for the ability to elicit guilt with a mere glance. I subconsciously placed my hand over my heart to check the frantic beating.

"You're not going to faint, are you?"

"No, I've been fighting a flu, that's all."

"Uh-huh."

"How is Paul connected?" I asked, trying to get the pressure off of me.

"You tell me."

I debated telling the detective about the detail I discovered—Paul snooping in Ed's work file—namely because it would put further suspicion on me. Maybe Detective Ricohr truly suspected me, or he was just pumping me for information. Either way I was in the middle of something, and it felt good.

"I don't have a clue," I said.

"Were he and Mr. Vadaresian close?"

"I doubt it. I don't think they even really knew each other. I'm responsible for overseeing Ed's group so he and Paul wouldn't have had much contact with each other outside of the coffee room."

"I was looking through Mr. Vadaresian's work emails," he said. "There was some interesting stuff in there."

"I doubt it," I told him.

"Really? So you've been snooping in there, too?"

"No, I doubt you were looking through his work emails," I corrected. "Any request would have to come through and be approved by me. And I don't have any recollection of someone from the police submitting such a request."

It felt good to counterpunch his assault. He had some information but it was limited and he needed me to fill in the blanks for him.

"So they are finally going to sell that building down in Lincoln Heights," he said.

"The Deakins?"

Detective Ricohr picked up on my surprise.

"I thought you were working with the Vadaresian family? They didn't tell you?"

"Who did you speak to?"

"You know I can't tell you that."

I hoped Rafi had heeded my advice and ceased this reckless pursuit to falsify documents and sell the building illegally. Apparently Detective Ricohr agreed.

"You may want to tell that kid not to do anything stupid."

We emerged from the bathroom to find Mike waiting for us with a big smile on his face. "So the rumors are true. The police academy bathroom *is* a hot spot for anonymous gay sex," he said before thrusting out his hand to introduce himself to Detective Ricohr. "Mike Wagner, nice to meet you."

"Alan Ricohr," the detective replied, enthusiastically shaking Mike's hand. I then watched Mike scramble to find a napkin to wipe off whatever was on his now-dampened hand.

"Touché, asshole," he laughed as Detective Ricohr sauntered out of the café.

GIRLS IN SUMMER DRESSES

The official part of the date lasted fifteen minutes. Cheli and I met at the Huntington Library, the former estate of a trolley car magnate and real estate developer at the turn of the twentieth century. His grounds were converted into a museum for his rare-book collection and exquisite gardens. For a mere twenty dollars, you could roam the estate and resent the wealth of someone who had died almost a hundred years ago.

Claire and I used to make a day of visiting the Huntington back in the early part of our relationship. She'd pack a gourmet picnic basket and I'd pretend to be interested in yet another variety of camellia bush. Who would have guessed there were more than fifty? The disturbing part of meeting Cheli there was that I had chosen the place. Perhaps subconsciously I was trying to re-create the relationship I had with Claire.

I arrived early and waited at the ticket booth. Cheli showed up a few minutes later and smiled warmly as she saw me. The confident detective owning her element at the precinct had transformed into the picture of femininity. The conservative pantsuit was replaced by a summer dress and sandals. She had straightened her hair and pulled it back to show off her slender neck and a diamond pendant. As she approached, she threw her arms out for a hug, and I was relieved we didn't have to go through the awkward moment of each deciding if it should be a hug or handshake greeting.

"What a beautiful day," she commented.

The conversation stayed at a water-cooler level, where weather and weekend plans reigned and were related with enthusiasm that didn't match the content. Like all good museumgoers, we lingered on the first few paintings we saw, all English portraits, dutifully read the information cards and absorbed the remarkable use of light and deft hand at re-creating the lace cuffs. We occasionally threw out a comment or two, something safe and most likely overheard from another patron. The more paintings we saw, the less we lingered. Then we skipped a painting or two, then whole rooms, and eventually we rushed through the museum like two people trying to find the bathroom.

At the main attraction, an original Gutenberg Bible, we milled about with the other gawkers to get a glimpse of this rarest of rare books. I glanced at the security guard standing a few paces off to the side. He was a middle-aged black man with watery eyes and graying sideburns. He kept his hands clasped behind his back as only a museum guard would do. Apparently, it was his job to make sure no one flipped through the Bible to his or her favorite psalm. But really there was nothing for him to do as the Bible was encased in what looked like bulletproof, UV-proof, everything-proof glass. His job then was to stand there for eight hours and do nothing. Although he was my height, he seemed shorter, like the great weight of boredom was ever so slightly pressing down on his shoulders in five-second intervals. He then looked up and caught me staring at him. He had a glazed look that screamed, "Shoot me!"

I turned to Cheli and was dismayed to see the same glazed look as the guard. And if there had been a mirror in the room, I am certain that same look would have stared back at me in my reflection.

"Let's get the hell out of here."

"Really?"

"Are you enjoying this?"

"Not at all," she said. She took my hand and led me out of the museum.

❊   ❊   ❊

We took my car and drove through the side streets of San Marino. As the Spanish estates melted away, so did the water-cooler talk, and we felt at ease for the first time that day. The conversation slipped back to what we were comfortable with, the only thing we really shared, which was Ed's disappearance. I filled Cheli in on the developments I had learned from Mike, leaving out any details involving Claire. She fixed her eyes on a distant spot in front of us as she processed the details, slightly nodding her head as she catalogued each piece of information. She reverted back to who she was, the detective. A detective in a yellow sundress.

"Is anything they did in building these low-income units illegal?"

"As disgusting as it sounds, it's all aboveboard."

"Then why kill Langford?"

"Or Ed?"

"We don't know for sure Mr. Vadaresian is dead," she corrected. "But for argument's sake, why kill him if it was an aboveboard deal that seemed to work for all sides? Langford was doing his deals and getting paid. Mr. Vadaresian was selling a building he wanted to sell and which sat for a long time on the market."

"Maybe they realized there was bigger money involved?"

"In what?" she asked.

Cheli was nosing around the issue I wanted to avoid, namely, the fact that Claire and McIntyre and presumably Valenti were somehow connected.

"These low-income housing community redevelopment projects can be big business."

"Says who?"

"My friend Mike Wagner."

She nodded her head, acknowledging the name.

"You know Mike?"

"Of him. He did a story on some officers on the GPD who were using DUI checkpoints as a way to get sexual favors from women caught up in the net. They'd threaten them with jail time but offered to let them go if they performed...acts on them. It burned the department pretty badly," she said, with disgust in her voice.

"Was it true?"

"I'm not mad at your friend," she explained, "but at the department. They put on a big dog-and-pony show, mandatory suspensions, closed-door investigations into misconduct, speeches in the paper. Then just sort of let the story die. They purposely drew it out until people lost interest. No one lost a job. One of them even got his shield before me," she added bitterly.

"That doesn't sound fair."

"Not much is for a woman on the force."

I could see her swallow the resentment.

"So where did you guys leave it?" she asked.

"Mike's following up on another lead. It could be just a coincidence, but a few months after the purchase of these buildings, there was another batch of transactions on an adjacent block to the properties we're talking about."

"More factory conversions into low-income housing?"

"Not really," I explained. "These were residential sales. Four-unit apartment complexes, single-family homes, et cetera. All bought within a month. All on the same block. All bought by the same person."

"Do you think it's connected?"

"Not sure. Mike said he was going to do some research on it, maybe talk to the owners."

"Why wait for Mike?" she quickly threw out.

I pulled my eyes from the road to study her.

"Seriously?"

"Why not?" she said, looking around at the neighborhood. "We're almost in Lincoln Heights already."

In all the talking, I had managed to drive us all the way through South Pas and Hermon and now skirted the bottom of Montecito Heights. Lincoln Heights was on the next bluff.

"You want to go knocking on doors on our first date?"

"It'll be fun," she laughed. "We can pretend to be partners. How's your Spanish?"

"*Yo conothzco español*," I said in my best Castilian accent, with a heavy lisp on the "z."

"They'll think you're a Mormon and slam the door in your face!"

MIRADA ARRASADORA

We parked on a dusty street a stone's throw from the Deakins Building and Carmen Hernandez's proposed new development. The block was unnaturally flat, like a giant bulldozer had smoothed the field and tamped out even the slightest deviation in the earth's surface. It produced a great leveling effect, where a person making morning coffee in one of the ramshackle row houses was at eye level with whomever happened to be strolling by out front.

The sun was intense and unobstructed. The only solace from its glare was the narrow strip of shade cast by the eight or so telephone poles that dotted the block. Standing in one of those shadows was an *abuelita* waiting for the local bus. She covered herself in a long skirt and a blouse that tied tightly at her wrists. She had a lizard-like stillness to her, as if any exertion would prove too much, and possibly give her away to whatever predator was lurking nearby.

"*Buenas tardes*," Cheli said and asked her if she lived

in the neighborhood. The old woman didn't answer right away. She studied Cheli, then looked at me, and grew even more suspicious. My sheepish wave didn't help ease her concern.

Cheli explained who she was and offered up her badge as proof of her identity. The *abuelita* studied the badge like it was a legal contract written in Sanskrit.

"Do you live in this neighborhood?" she asked again in Spanish.

"*Sí*," the old woman answered.

Cheli showed her the list of sales on the paper Mike had provided. The *abuelita* brightened and pointed to one of the addresses. She then emerged from her spot in the shade and started rambling in Spanish, directing it all toward me.

"I don't understand," I pleaded, which did nothing to slow the onslaught. "Cheli, why is she talking to me?"

"She thinks you're the police," she explained.

"Me?"

"And I'm your…translator."

Discrimination was often perpetuated the most by one's own people.

"Tell her I'm not the police. *No soy policia*," I tried.

"She won't listen," she answered and reluctantly stepped into the role of translator.

"She says she has lived here for over twelve years. They don't make any trouble and no one bothers them. It's just her and her daughter-in-law and her grand-children. She works over in Cypress Park at a shipping company. She says she is legally here—"

"It's okay," I told the woman, "we aren't interested in that."

The *abuelita* smiled as Cheli translated. She then said something to Cheli that made her blush. Cheli tried to pass it off but the old woman kept at her.

"What's going on?" I asked.

"Nothing," Cheli replied.

"Clearly something is being said."

Cheli shrugged. "She tells me I need a man like you."

The old woman stroked my arm and spoke into my eyes.

"She says you are kind and strong and—"

"And what?"

"You, um, have *mirada arrasadora*."

"Which means what?"

"Bedroom eyes."

"I usually get 'smoldering,' but bedroom eyes isn't bad."

"You realize you are preening like a peacock after being hit on by an eighty-year-old woman."

"The old ones know from experience. Maybe you should listen to your elders."

Cheli interrupted the lovefest to pump the old lady for more information. There was an issue several months back when some men showed up at her door and started asking a lot of questions about her immigration status. Apparently the earlier part about being legal wasn't entirely accurate. Her grandchildren were legal, having been born in the States, but she and her daughter-in-law were undocumented.

"Were these immigration officials?" I asked.

"ICE?" the old woman repeated. "No, no, not ICE."

"What did they want with you?" Cheli asked.

The *abuelita* explained that these men threatened to turn them in to the authorities. They somehow knew, or guessed, she was not in the country legally. They also knew she had her family and warned her that she was putting her grandchildren at risk of losing their mother and grandmother.

"So now we have vigilante immigration officers?" I said.

The old woman went on to explain that these men said they would leave her alone if she did them a favor.

"What kind of favor?"

The woman's response appeared to puzzle Cheli.

"What'd she say?" I asked.

"They told her to stop paying her rent."

We heard a similar story at several of the other properties in question. Most involved some sort of threat—either exposing the occupants' immigration status or just the good old-fashioned violent kind of threat. Those who were told to stop paying their rent were also told that these same men would protect them if the landlord tried to get tough with them.

Evicting renters from a property is a long, drawn-out affair involving court orders, US marshals, and endless documentation. Many deadbeat tenants manage to hang on for months after the initial request to vacate. In the poorer neighborhoods where the oversight was lax and the participants were largely unaware of their rights, the eviction process was often much faster and much nastier. It mostly involved a new set of locks, your belongings piled on the sidewalk, and a German shepherd on the stoop in case you got any bright ideas about returning.

Clearly, the men who threatened the abuelita and the other residents knew how the landlords would retaliate. The question then was why go through all this trouble. Talking to one of building owners gave us the reason why.

This particular landlord was the proud owner of a building that didn't strive to one day be a called a dump. The carpets were stained and rank, the windows grimy and cracked and in some cases missing the panes entirely. Dark corners of rooms were darkened further by patches of mold that contributed to the sour air and tickled the back of the throat.

He was that rare breed of fat man who was neither jolly nor gentle. A cheap oscillating fan in his office gave us a whiff of diabetes and deodorant soap with each pass. His leg was propped up on a stool, his knee a leaky mess, crisscrossed with surgical scars and pink circles where fluids were drained. Empathy for his physical suffering only partly offset the anger I had for how he treated the people living in his buildings.

"They told me if I went to the police, I'd never walk again," the man explained. "So I went to the police anyway. They shattered my kneecap. They hit me ten times in the same spot. They were right about the not-walking part," he added.

"What'd they want from you?" asked Cheli.

"This building. First they tell everyone to stop paying rent and they put the squeeze on me. They know I need the money. It's my only income. But I'm a stubborn bastard. I don't budge easy. A few weeks later there's these guys again with a few friends in my living room. I told them I'd sell. They accepted the offer but gave me a beating anyway."

"I assume you didn't get a fair price." I said.

"What do you think?" he said. "Now I got to figure out

what to do when the money I got from the sale runs out."

"Can you describe the men?" I asked.

"Nothing special," he replied. "Just your regular set of Armos."

Cheli and I shared a look.

"They were Armenians," I stated.

Cheli pulled up a series of mug shots on her smart phone, the same ones she had me look through after the incident at the tire shop. The man picked out a few.

"These guys all look the same," he said, laughing.

But then he settled on one picture.

"This is the guy. He's the one who told me what to do." He held up the phone. On it was a photo of the hook-nosed, junior Vor, Ardavan Temekian.

✺   ✺   ✺

As the sun started to slip behind the hill, we stopped off at a crowded Mexican seafood joint and split a goblet of shrimp in a spicy tomato broth. We chased it down with cans of Tecate dipped in lime juice and salt. Overhead, clear bags of water and vinegar hung from the rafters, apparently to keep the flies away, but it didn't seem to be working, as the buzzing of wings nearly drowned out the busy street.

"Is that supposed to get rid of the flies or attract them?" I asked.

"My mom used to put out a bag of ammonia to keep stray cats from peeing on the grass in front of our house."

"Did it work?"

"About as well as it is with these flies."

A few sips of Tecate brought more of those stories out of Cheli. Her parents were first-generation Mexican

Americans from a small barrio outside Mazatlán. "Shrimp was a big part of my childhood," she said, laughing. After the age of six she was pretty much raised by her mother. Her father didn't up and disappear as much as he sort of drifted away. One night away from the house turned into two. Soon he was more houseguest than family member, but the kind of houseguest you actually wanted to stay longer. There was another woman, but Cheli didn't think that was an accurate description. "There was more than just one." She smiled when she said that, but there was pain behind it.

Cheli had a brother who never amounted to much of anything unless you put stock in extended stays at Lompoc. They were all minor infractions, but eventually they added up into a long sentence.

"*El Principe* sure knows how to find trouble."

"Doesn't sound like a prince."

"In my mom's eyes, he'll always be the Prince," she said. "Let's just say in a Latino family, the men can do no wrong. Not that I am bitter or anything!"

"I'm not so sure that's unique to Latinos."

"But we have a special way of putting men on pedestals."

"Then you must be the prodigal child, *Detective* Alvarado."

"You would think," she shot back. I could tell she no longer wanted to talk about it. It sounded like she was in that vortex we all fall into of perpetually trying to please the people who turn us away. She quickly changed the subject.

"I want you to be more careful. The AP can be ruthless when they have to. I know you find this detective stuff interesting, but this isn't a game."

"I never said it was."

"I think you need to step aside and let me run with it."

She must have seen the disappointment on my face. I had never felt so alive as I did these past few weeks. To willingly walk away from it was going to be hard. Cheli tenderly reached out and touched my arm. "I also don't want to see you get hurt."

"Okay," I said. "I'll step aside."

By the time we got back to the Huntington parking lot it was after dark and the guard at the gate was about to lock Cheli's car in for the night. Los Angeles has this incredible ability to scald you during the day with relentless sunlight, but at night, as soon as that sun slips over the horizon, the air turns cool and quiet.

I felt goose bumps on Cheli's arm as I took hold of her hand. We silently leaned in and kissed, a little awkwardly at first, but it felt comforting to have someone in my arms again. As she pulled away and got into her car, I heard her whisper, "*Mirada arrasadora.*"

THE STEAMER INCIDENT

Tuesday morning brought a new chapter to my Human Resources career. A regional manager for distribution returned to work after a long weekend only to discover that her office had been vandalized. This type of incident was rare to the corporate setting and warranted senior manager–level involvement due to the nature of the vandalism. As my co-manager, Paul, was out with his typical "eye problem" after a three-day weekend (he couldn't see himself working after such a nice, long weekend), the investigation into the affair landed in my lap.

The first thing I did was pull the key card logs from the weekend, starting with Friday night. Every associate has a badge with his or her photo. More importantly, they have a chip that grants them access to and from every section of the building, including the parking garage. A computer logs all of the time stamps and keeps it for three years. These logs have proved invaluable in theft investigations and when building a case for termination against an associate. Between a computer log and key card log, we were able to piece together sone-one's entire day, from what favorite gossip sites they frequented to the number of bathroom breaks they took.

It didn't take long to narrow it down to a single suspect, though the name surprised even me. The associate in question was the administrative assistant to the woman whose office was vandalized.

She was also a thirty-year vet to the organization and quite possibly the gentlest human soul ever to grace this land. She organized the annual Adopt-A-Family charity event that provided essentials to needy families around the holidays. And she'd quietly fill the funding gap out of her own pocket for all the chumps who "forgot" to pay their five dollars for the privilege to wear jeans on Fridays. She held a free knitting class during lunch on Wednesdays, baked homemade cakes for every monthly birthday celebration, decorated cubicles for associate anniversaries, and even volunteered for the job no one wanted, which was floor warden during earthquake evacuation drills, a job that ensured—in the event of an actual earthquake—she'd be the last person out of the building. Knowing all this, I was hard-pressed to believe, despite the mounting evidence against her, that this sweet little lady would come into the office early on a Saturday morning to defecate on the chair of her direct report.

I brought the woman into my office for some "fact finding." By all appearances, the suspect showed no signs of guilt. She was her usual cheerful self and even remembered that last week was my twenty-third anniversary with the firm. I didn't want to let on that she was our person of interest in the case and began my questioning in a breezy fashion.

"Oh my goodness," she started characteristically, "what a thing to do. I can't fathom someone from this company doing that. It's simply tragic."

"Yes, very tragic."

The woman recapped the morning in concise detail. When she got to the part of the discovery of the excrement, she took a few moments to gather herself. The words did not come easily and appeared to visibly upset her.

"The poor thing let out a scream. I must admit, I feared the worst."

"Worse than what was sitting on her chair?"

"I thought...she may have lost a loved one," she said and made the sign of the cross. "It was that kind of scream."

"You work closely with Ms. Timmons. Can you think of any incidents that we should be aware of? Any conflicts she may have had with other associates?"

"I can't imagine anyone at the company doing such a thing."

"I know, you said that earlier. But even small things can lead to larger consequences. People we think we know are capable of doing things we never thought possible."

I thought I saw her eye twitch, or was it a twinkle?

"Not anyone I know. And I know people."

"What's it like working for Ms. Timmons?"

"Ms. Timmons?" she repeated as if there were some confusion on who we were talking about. "She's a smart woman, very dedicated. Even when she's not in the office I can see she's logged on from home."

"And working with her? What's that like?"

"Fine. No real issues." It felt like there was more; it just needed some time to be coaxed out. "Sure, she can be particular at times about the process, but we're all in this together and in the end we get the work done, which is what really matters."

And there it was—the root of the issue.

"Does she micromanage?"

"Goodness, no. I didn't mean to imply that." Micromanagement was a criticism commonly levied against most mid-level managers. "Really, it's about finding that balance in styles. It all works out in the end."

It was the second time she used the phrase "in the end," like there was some inevitable outcome that was beyond her control, one she had to either accept willingly or unwillingly.

"Is she fair?"

"Yes, she's very clear in what she asks us."

"And in what she asks of you?"

"We've struck that right balance in approaches."

"And on how you're evaluated?"

"Very consistently."

She had the right answers but to questions I wasn't asking. The woman's mounting frustration was palpable. She began this manic gesture with her hand, touching her thumb with each of her fingers—pinkie first, then ring finger, middle, and finally index—and then start it all over again. She did it with an obsessive-compulsive rhythm.

One of the dirty secrets in corporate America was this: the good never go unpunished. This administrative assistant was a dynamo, an individual who truly helped make the place run. And to reward her for her good work, she was transferred to Ms. Timmons, a woman whose "approach" had alienated half of the company and run through at least ten administrative assistants over the last seven years. Most either quit or were terminated. And rather than solve the issue head-on by going to the root of the problem, it was decided that a valuable asset like this sweet administrative assistant sitting before me be thrust into the hell that was working with Ms. Timmons.

Old-fashioned harassment—the pat-on-the-ass kind once common—was rare and all but extinct in Corporate America. What cropped up in its place was a more insidious form of harassment that was just as harmful as it was totally legal. This new form was an ultra–passive aggressiveness, meted out in a way that remained within the rules of the company and always with a smile.

Take a simple mistake like printing up the wrong handout for a meeting. A normal person would simply correct your mistake and ask for the right handout. A normal jerk would call you a "dumbass" and then ask for the right handout. Ms. Timmons would do something different. She'd most likely start like this:

"I noticed you printed the wrong handout for the meeting." She'd wear an expression of honest-to-goodness concern. Then she'd say, "Did you mean to print the wrong handout?" That question alone has no merit, as only a total nincompoop would willfully make a mistake like that. But what it does is force you to answer the question. It wouldn't end there. "Are there any issues you are dealing with that led to this mistake?" Again, this is all aboveboard. If brought to HR, Ms. Timmons could claim she was trying to identify any obstructions to the associate's ability to do quality work. Although your answer would be that there were no issues and that it wouldn't happen again, she would recommend you take a time-management course (God help you if you declined, as this would show an unwillingness to develop) and now you are sentenced to an eight-hour seminar with some hack from a corporate consulting firm. Have this done to you all day, every day and you too might revert to your pure animal instincts and take a dump on someone's ergonomic chair.

I watched the woman do her nervous finger dance and I was overcome with a great sadness because I had contributed to this mess. All my work in HR had enabled people like Ms. Timmons to exact their torture on people who couldn't defend themselves. My job was to protect those people and here I was an accomplice in their dirty work.

I don't know what came over me but I reached out and took hold of the woman's hand. I could still feel her fingers continue their incessant tapping but I slowly squeezed her hand and they eventually stopped.

She knew that I knew, but it didn't matter. I closed the case as unsolved and set about a plan to transfer the unnamed administrative assistant to a more accommodating position.

I also decided to question Claire about what we had discovered. I had been avoiding a confrontation with her in the hopes that things would just reconcile naturally. But that was never going to happen.

Despite whatever promise I made to Cheli, I needed to keep pressing.

IT'S MUTUAL

As an attorney, Claire was skilled at answering questions without ever giving answers, so I decided to confront her directly in the hopes of getting a visceral reaction. Calling ahead only gave her time to work up a response, so I planned to drop by her office unannounced.

I took a shortcut through the Bonaventure Hotel and prepared what I was going to say. I must have been nervous because after five minutes I realized I still wasn't out of the hotel. With its maze-like structure of half loops and symmetrical concrete cylinders I felt like a hamster running in place on a Venn diagram. I finally found my way out of the rabbit hole and skirted down Flower, under the 4th Street overpass where the city's bike messengers gathered to smoke dope when they weren't being bothered to actually having to make a delivery.

The elevator spat me out on the top floor with panoramic views of downtown. The reception desk was staffed by a very attractive woman with green eyes and a low-cut blouse that had the power of an industrial magnet.

The general rule for office "eye candy": the film industry and real estate firms took it seriously; everyone else hired your great-aunt from Pacoima.

"I'm here to see Claire Courtwright," I told the young woman.

"Do you have an appointment?" she asked.

"Yes, she told me to swing by when I made it downtown. I'm her husband," I added.

The receptionist's cool tone immediately changed. Nothing was more desirable than someone who belongs to someone you looked up to. She gobbled up the phone and enthusiastically called Claire's office.

"She'll be right out," the girl announced cheerfully.

I sidled over to the waiting lounge with its clean-lined sofas and glass coffee table. Knowing where their bread was buttered, one of the magazines featured a cover story on Valenti's philanthropic work. He clearly didn't adhere to Maimonides's Eight Levels of Charity, which values anonymous giving. For every dollar Valenti gave to a worthy cause he spent three more dollars publicly promoting how generous he was.

Every Sunday he took out a full-page ad in the *Times* to thank himself for all the great work he was doing. The ads featured a dozen or so heads of local nonprofits who had benefitted from Valenti's largesse. All the participants looked like they had been forced at gunpoint to utter the quotes attributed to them in the captions below their faces. Everyone on the page was extremely grateful but it didn't seem like they had much of a choice.

"This is a surprise," Claire said behind me.

She looked good in her business suit and hair neatly pulled back in a clasp. The receptionist secretly eyed us while feigning interest in her computer screen.

"Do you have a minute to talk?" I asked.

"Not really," Claire said and checked her watch. "Is something wrong?"

"I want to talk over a couple of things."

"You're acting suspicious."

"Come on, let's go grab a coffee."

Claire reluctantly agreed after looking back to her office like there was some personification of "work" tapping his watch and reminding her of her duties.

"I'm just stepping out," she said to the receptionist. "I'll be back in a few."

We grabbed lattes at the coffee stand in the lobby of the building. I tried to form the words in my head but it was hard to concentrate. The marbled floors, walls, and pillars made it hard to hear anything. All the voices around us merged into a single, incomprehensible echo. The barista banging used grinds from the machine didn't help.

"Say that again," I asked, "I can't hear you."

"Don't make me repeat it."

"Seriously, I didn't hear you. What did you say?"

She looked annoyed.

"Claire, I didn't hear you with all this noise. Please repeat what you said."

"I want a divorce," she blurted out.

The skin tingled in my face and arms and I felt the blood suddenly pumping through my body.

"Okay, I heard it that time. Jesus…really?"

"I think it's the best thing for us."

"I'd ask that you refrain from making judgments about 'us' without first conferring with me."

"Don't be a nit."

"Nice, I get delivered this news at a shitty coffee cart in a crowded lobby and then get called names because I don't like it."

"You know it isn't going to work—"

"No, no I don't know that. And stop making up my mind for me."

"*I* know it isn't going to work."

It was just like Claire—here I came to confront her about her questionable involvement in the dealings around the Deakins Building, Langford's murder, and Ed's disappearance and she undercuts me with her announcement.

"Are you seeing someone?"

"Stop."

"That tool bag from Valenti's office, I assume. Boy, you're really making a name for yourself."

She didn't justify my barb by responding to it. She had the quiet equilibrium of a person who had already thought the entire thing through to its very last move. I secretly cursed myself for coming down here. I knew all along this was the unavoidable outcome of our separation and yet I had avoided it as long as I could.

"I didn't want to hurt you, Chuck," she said, placing her hand over mine. Taking the high ground was easy when you know you're the one walking away a stronger person. I mustered the composure to play the same game.

"You're right, Claire. I'm sorry for what I said." I placed my other hand over hers so we now had that two-fisted handshake sales guys like to do to prove they care. I then gave that extra squeeze to show how serious I was. She may have taken the high ground, but I took the goddamned bluff above it.

Her eyes started to well up and we stayed locked in that "embrace" for what seemed like an hour.

"I'm happy that we can get through this amicably," she said, which was code for "let's not make a scene."

That part I didn't agree to.

KNIGHTS ERRANT
OF THE PURPLE CRUSADERS

The ascendency of football to the title of "America's game" coincided with a rash of football analogies in the workplace. We no longer managed a project. We worked on "moving the ball down the field." And when the project went awry, someone invariably called an "audible." Never had so many balls been "put through the uprights," so many "chin straps" been buckled, so many "timeouts" called than over the last year in my office. Luckily, the other true football tradition of towel slapping didn't catch on. When Easy Mike and I "huddled up" to "run the Xs and Os" on the board of the Deakins game, we threw out those tired gridiron phrases and went old school—we convened in the War Room.

The War Room was actually just a corner of Mike's office with a dry-erase board and an endless supply of colored markers and Post-it notes. We created a DNA map of the case, the nucleus of which was a circle around Ed's name. We added all of the players—Claire, Valenti, Temekian, Ashry-whatever-his-name-was, and anyone who might be involved—and then drew lines from names where we knew there was a connection. The line was labeled with whatever information we had. So Claire's bubble and Langford's had a note that they brokered deals together. Anything we didn't know was marked with a question mark. The result was a dizzying web of facts, potential facts, and missing facts.

"This Temekian character confuses me," Mike said as he tapped a printout of his mug shot. "He's telling Ed's kid to sell the building even though Ed is missing. We know he talked to Ed near the day he disappeared. We also know he's going around threatening people in this block of Holcomb Street, a stone's throw from the Deakins Building, and forcing them to sell the buildings on the cheap. One thing we don't know is this."

He wrote a new name on the board.

"Who is Salas?" I asked.

Salas, Mike explained, was the name listed on all of the transactions on Holcomb Street where Temekian and his thugs pressured the owners into selling. "So we have a mysterious guy buying up an entire block," I said.

"I've seen this kind of thing before over in Hollywood during the revitalization movement," Mike said. "Developers snatched up parcels of land under some shell corporation to keep the speculators off their track. They didn't want to tip their hand too early, until they had secured all the land they needed. The last thing they needed was some opportunist grabbing a plot and then holding them over a barrel."

"Is this something Valenti might do?" I asked.

"He perfected the technique. His work is particularly hard to piece together. It's like a shell game—the ball is never where you think it is."

"This one seems too simple, then. We got a name, an actual person, not a series of phony corporations."

"We got a name, but we don't know if this is a real person," Mike corrected.

"Well, there must be an address on the transaction paperwork. Let's go see who he is."

"*He* is a rental box out in Van Nuys, at a place whose owner has standards. Fifty bucks couldn't get him to give me any information on the box renter."

"Let's stake out the place and see who picks up the mail," I suggested.

"That could take weeks. And they may never actually check it."

"We could ask the police."

"Screw them."

"But they could get a warrant to find out the rental box owner," I reasoned.

"I don't want them nosing in on our story. They're doing their job—a poor one, I might add—and we're doing ours."

"Okay, I just don't want us to get mixed up with them. Obstruction of justice is a felony."

"I didn't know you were an Eagle Scout. What are you nervous about, that clown detective we met at the Police Academy?"

"No, the other one."

"What other one? That broad from Glendale?"

"Go easy, Mike. She wants to help with the case. She told me to be careful and to let her handle it."

"Yeah, and steal our credit. No thanks. This is ours," he said, pounding the table. "No chick wanting to make lieutenant is going to take it from us."

Crass as he was, I appreciated his drive, even if it cut a little close to the bone. Of course, Mike didn't dabble in scalpels. He preferred the machete.

"Why are you talking to this Glendale detective anyway?"

"No reason," I stammered, "we're just kind of getting to know each other."

"Claire's out, this new girl is in. I love it." He laughed. "Resentment and revenge—the two great motivators. Well, at least I know you're committed!" He slapped me on the back, too hard. "Okay, how are you going to get information on what your ex-wife is working on?"

❄ ❄ ❄

Bunker Hill was more of a plateau than a hill. The monstrous bases to the skyscrapers that ringed it served as sheer, impenetrable bastions. The "ground" floor was actually four or five stories up, where developers had flattened the crest of the natural hill and created an undisturbed oasis of plazas, water fountains, and public gardens.

The design was deliberate—they wanted to keep the riffraff at the bottom of the hill from mingling with the legions of corporate workers at the top. If a homeless man somehow navigated the maze up to the top of the hill, a purple-shirted downtown security force funded by the local businesses would quickly escort him back to his rightful spot at the bottom.

In the shadows of my building was a grassless stretch of dirt under an overpass where one segment of the riffraff hung out—the city's bike messengers. They used this spot to fill out paperwork while waiting for the next call, and when no call came, to smoke enough dope to give pedestrians across the street a contact high.

I had called around to the various messenger outfits and pretended to be from Claire's office until I found a voice that recognized the name as a client. I then invented some story about a holiday bonus and needing to know the name of our guy so we could personalize the card.

"You mean Rosie?" the voice on the phone asked.

Apparently, our guy was a gal.

"That's a woman?" I shot back, which got a good chuckle out of the dispatcher. "Good God, all this time I thought she was a he."

"She sure acts like one," he told me.

As I approached, a group of messengers perched on the back half of a park bench eyed me suspiciously. There was a code among this set that went beyond the standard look of the hipster shirt and calf-high cargo pants, and was in direct contrast to my corporate code. These messengers were the urban esthetes, living a stripped-down existence for which perpetual motion and the camaraderie of their peers were all that mattered. They viewed me as the life they rejected, with my starched shirt and luxury sedan, which they enjoyed cutting off on their daily routes. Many of these kids were from wealthy families; some were college educated, and none felt the need to help me in the least.

"Never heard of her," one of them shot back.

"It's important that I speak to her," I said.

"I'm sure it is," said an older messenger with half-dollar-size disks in his earlobes. Seeing the stretched skin made me queasy. "But she's not here," he said and headed off on a delivery.

As he left, I saw him subtly glance over my right shoulder to a group by the 4th Street ramp. It was an obvious tell, but I didn't think he meant to give her away.

I approached the group of ten, of which there were three women, and tossed out a casual, "Hey, Rosie."

A young woman, mid-twenties with a bob cut, jerked her head in my direction. She dressed like a man, wore her hair like a man, but her eyes were feminine. They were soft and green and led you to believe she'd make a good mother. When she saw me approaching, she subtly slipped a small ceramic pipe into her pocket.

"Do you have a minute to talk?" I asked.

"Maybe," she said. "What do you want?"

"Can we go for a walk?"

"How'd you get my name?" she asked warily.

"From your dispatcher," I told her.

This seemed to put her at ease. She grabbed her messenger bag and led the way over to the far recesses of the underpass. As I walked behind her I noticed the large tattoos of hula girls on both her calves.

"He usually gives me a heads-up before sending people over," she said. "What do you need?"

"I was wondering if you could do me a favor."

"A favor?" she said, laughing. "I'll do you a big favor

depending on how much money you got."

"Oh," I said, a little confused. "I have money."

"Then let's talk."

"You do deliveries for Jenkins Hollister Grubb, right?"

"Sometimes, but I share that route with another guy."

"What would it take for you to bring me any packages that go between that office and another office over on Olympic?"

Her face blanched and her eyes narrowed.

"You want me to do what?"

"I'll pay you for it."

"I don't want your goddamn money," she fumed.

"But you just said you'd do it for the money—"

"I thought you were buying weed!"

Rosie grabbed her bag and stormed off back to her group. I shouted out to her, "So dealing marijuana is okay but borrowing a few documents is not? I'm glad you have your priorities straight!"

She reeled around to face me. "Don't talk to me about morals—you dickwads may control the economy, but you don't control me."

The main beneficiaries of the economic recovery were the very people who started the financial crisis in the first place. Underneath were legions of very bitter people.

"Slow down on the rhetoric, Rosie. I'm not part of the one percent. I'm just a regular guy who makes an okay living and needs some information."

"Well, you're not going to get it from me."

The hula girls danced on her calves as she stalked off.

"That went well," I said to myself.

As I turned to head back up the ramp, I heard a commotion over by Flower Street, where a growing group of bike messengers was being confronted by a handful of the purple-shirted downtown security team. They were mostly wannabe cops who took their role of safeguarding the area's streets a little too seriously. "The less authority, the greater the asshole," Mike used to intone.

These Purple Crusaders rode around on top-of-the-line mountain bikes, even though this area under the overpass was the only patch of dirt in all of downtown. They wore black cargo pants, which they tucked into their spit-shined jackboots. They had utility belts like the average patrolman but, naturally, no guns. The shirt of choice was a two-sizes-too-small, dual-layered Lycra piece with the word SECURITY screaming on the back. The fitting conclusions to the ensemble were mirrored, wraparound sunglasses.

"You're going to have to vacate the premises," a Purple Crusader announced. All of his banter came from TV police procedurals.

"Go fuck yourself," my ear-gauged friend responded, recently returned from a delivery.

The security member pulled the mini-microphone clipped to his collar closer to his mouth. "Six-forty-two, requesting backup to Flower and 4th."

"I don't care how many of you come down here," the messenger shouted. "I'll piss on all of you."

That got a big laugh from the group.

"Sir, did you just threaten me?"

"No, sir, I didn't threaten you," the guy softened. "I threatened *all* of you pussies!"

"You do realize that threatening me or a member of my team is a felony," the guard explained, just as five more of his team came riding up. They stood upright on just one of the pedals so as to quickly dismount in case there was trouble. Also, it would look silly using a kickstand when you were trying to be taken seriously.

"Dude, you're just a punk with nothing better to do now that the Occupy Wall Street protests are over."

That one stung. The protests were at least seven years old but were still held up as the Purple Crusaders' finest moment. At the height of the protests, the lobby of my building was "occupied" for a few hours while the great unwashed tried to set up camp. They got washed a few minutes later when building security turned the sprinklers on as they pitched tents in the green space out front.

In the end, it was all sound and no fury. Security outnumbered the rabble two-to-one. The real cops looked bored but content to collect triple time as they followed the group from building to building. For the Purple Crusaders, however, it was the event of a lifetime. They saw themselves as the last line of defense between anarchy and the civilized world. Little did they know that the people they were protecting were angrier at the Purple Crusaders than the protesters for making them use the back exit and having to walk an extra block to get to their favorite sandwich shop at lunchtime.

Despite the wrap-around sunglasses, I could see a twitch in the head guard's eye. He didn't appreciate the insult to his group's honor. It was time for him to pull rank and prove what kind of power he really had.

"Six-forty-two," he said flatly into his microphone,

"requesting police backup. Code eighty-three—threat to a peace officer."

Even the bike messengers knew this meant a serious escalation to the situation. Part of the deal brokered between the downtown security force and the real force was a mutual support clause. Cops, although reluctantly, viewed any threat to a Purple Crusader as a threat to their own.

"Come on, dude," said the main instigator. "You're calling the cops? No one threatened nobody."

"You said it yourself," he replied. "I believe you referred to us as a derogatory term for the female genitalia."

Snickers emanated from the back of the messenger group and from my own lips. I decided to step in and defuse the situation.

"Listen, guys, there's no need for threats, and there's no need to call the police," I said. "Both sides are wrong here. You got a little poisonous with the name calling," I told the bike messenger. "And you guys were a little quick to escalate the situation," I said to the security team. "Let's just accept this and move on."

There was a long pause between the warring sides as my words sunk in. Perhaps all those years of conflict resolution training had its benefits outside the office after all.

"I'll move on," said a voice behind me, "after you accept this, bitch!" Rosie flew past my shoulder and landed a clean right hook on the head guard's chin. His legs buckled and he went down on one knee. The punch sparked a full-blown melee, with me stuck in the middle.

I got spun around to the ground and was nearly trampled as the two sides converged over me. Few punches were thrown, but there was a hell of a lot of shouting, shoving, and name-calling. The police sirens grew louder, and the bike messengers decided it was time to vacate the premises like they were originally asked. Clashing tires and gnashing chains crisscrossed the area as messengers melted into the evening traffic. Out of a cloud of dust, a bike skidded a few inches from my head. Rosie smiled down on me with those soft eyes.

"A hundred bucks per delivery," she said and flicked her card at me.

B&E

The house was located in Beachwood Canyon, a veined scramble of roads pumping out of old Hollywood and reaching far up into the hills below the iconic sign. Most of the streets twisted into the canyon's many crevices, narrowing as the elevation grew until they were just thin slits barely wide enough for one car to pass. There were no three-point turns in Beachwood Canyon.

The houses clung to whatever land they could grab without falling into the ravine below, and when there was no suitable land they'd built elaborate stilts that cantilevered the entire place fifty feet off the ground. My house was a modest ranch that we had redone over the years. It was worth far more than it warranted. If a tornado somehow picked it up and dumped it in a beautiful community in Illinois or Oregon or upstate New York, it would immediately lose at least a million dollars in value.

Our house was dug into the hillside on a lot that sloped down from the road and as such offered an inauspicious first impression of a shingled roof and a satellite dish. Once you walked down a short flight of stairs and into the house, however, you were treated to a beautiful view of the lights of East Hollywood and, way off in the distance, the skyscrapers of downtown.

The house was dark except for the hall light, which was always on. Wednesday nights were GNO (Girls Night Out) for Claire and her friends. They were most likely splitting a bottle of pinot at some trendy restaurant, but I wanted to make sure, so I drove slowly by the house in case I saw any movement inside. Our street wasn't one you drove through, so I made only one pass. Any kind of cruising around would immediately draw suspicion. I looped back and parked down the street in case Claire or any busybody neighbors recognized my car.

It was very quiet as I made my way down the front steps. I rang the doorbell just to be sure no one was there. Hearing nothing, I slid my key into the lock. It only got halfway.

"She changed the locks?" I breathed to myself. Unless Claire had paid for twenty-four-hour locksmith services, this divorce had been in the works for some time. I tried to figure out another way into the house. Mike was right—resentment is a great motivator.

The house was alarmed, and if Claire had changed the locks on the doors she had certainly changed the code to the alarm. The last thing I wanted was to trip that system and have Claire, and the police, get a notice that someone was breaking into the house. Then I remembered one of the arguments we'd had earlier in the year.

Claire was a stickler about natural light. "Why live in LA if you are going to sit in the dark?" she would say.

Although our house had an expansive southern exposure out the back, the front of the house was fairly dark, as it bumped up into the hillside and was encased by retaining walls that kept the earth from washing us away during the next big rainstorm. No matter how many lamps, hanging fixtures, or LED strips we bought, Claire still complained it was too dark and insisted on putting in a skylight. I fought it; she won. Since the skylight was installed after the alarm system was put in, the unit itself was not linked to the circuit. And Claire always forgot to lock it, despite my numerous reminders.

I went around to the side of the house and climbed onto the retaining wall, now slick with ice plant and ivy. It was a simple step onto the roof and three more steps to the open skylight. I unhinged the latch and pried the bubble open. It was situated right above our bed, which was the root of another argument we had after installation when I was awoken at six in the morning by a searing ray of light reserved for epiphanies. I double-checked that the bed was empty. The thought of jumping down onto Claire, and someone else, gave me the shudders.

It looked quiet, so I jumped down and was met with the stiff resistance of a memory-foam mattress. I rolled off the bed and drifted through the house in the dark. Muscle memory guided me around sharp-edged coffee tables and over rugs that had started to curl up in spots. Nothing had changed since I'd moved out, and yet it felt different. This house that I had built—or at least hired a contractor and interior designer to renovate—was no longer mine, a reverse déjà vu in which everything looked familiar yet nothing felt it. Things that I had bought or hung or sat on were all still exactly where I had left them, but they had lost all traces of me. It felt feminine, like the house had undergone a sex-change operation in the few months since I had moved out. And tromping through it in the dark gave me the unseemly feeling that I was violating it.

I found Claire's laptop in the living room and powered it up. It'd be better if I had her iPhone, but that would have to be surgically removed from her hand. Luckily, Claire was a Mac snob and insisted on using her home computer for work-related stuff because she did not like using PCs. She also used the same password for all of her sites. It was the name of her childhood imaginary friend and the year she graduated from high school. A psychologist could have a field day with that.

I pulled up her personal email and waded through thousands of shopping emails, sale announcement emails, coupon emails, and more shopping emails. Claire had to be on every e-blast list in the greater Los Angeles area. Ninety-five percent of her time spent communicating was filtering out all of the noise around the one or two personal emails in her box, and it didn't seem to bother her. Claire had embraced the digital age, while I tried to hide from it. I once tried to get the username "UNSUBSCRIBE" for my personal email, but unfortunately it was already taken.

I sorted the emails by sender and scrolled down until I got to Todd McIntyre. There were several emails, but the most intriguing was a long string with the word "ARROYO" in the subject line. An arroyo is a creek bed or wash. The common reference in Los Angeles was the Arroyo Seco—dry riverbed—that ran through

Pasadena, skirted downtown, and had the country's first freeway running parallel to it. A quick scan of the emails led me to believe the Arroyo was some sort of development Claire was helping McIntyre with. The real arroyo was somewhat close to the set of buildings in the Deakins area, but not close enough to make a direct connection. It just seemed too much of a coincidence, so I forwarded all of the emails to my personal account and then went into the "sent" folder to delete any record of this transaction.

Just as I was about to shut down the computer, I noticed another string of emails to McIntyre but sent to a different email address. The former were to his work email but the latter were clearly to his personal. They had subject lines like "This weekend" and names of restaurants and the one that made me feel queasy, "Last night." I resisted the urge to read them. Instead, I sorted them by date to find out when the first email to the personal account was sent, which should mark the beginning of their affair. I needed to know how long it had been going on.

I was surprised to learn that the affair didn't begin while Claire and I were living together. It started a fair amount of time after the separation, but that only made me feel worse. Somehow it was less upsetting to know that Claire left me for someone else than to learn that she simply no longer wanted me.

I suddenly felt deflated. I passed on the idea of exiting through the skylight and just walked out the front door. The alarm wailed in the quiet night but luckily no one was interested in investigating the cause.

CHOLOS LIKE DOO-WOP

It was late by the time I got back to my apartment in Lincoln Heights. I'd stopped off at a burger joint in Hollywood just to be around people. I ordered a double cheeseburger with fries and a beer but only drank the beer. I ordered two more beers and then decided if I was going to get soused I might as well do it at home, where it was cheaper and I didn't have to worry about a DUI checkpoint. I grabbed a bottle out of the refrigerator and decided to drink it right there in the kitchen and nearly downed most of it in the first few gulps. My neighbor was at it again.

> I fell for you and I knew
> The vision of your love-loveliness...

The old ones had a way of catching me off guard with their plaintive voices longing for that loved one who had left and gone or never showed up in the first place. And as if sensing my need to wallow in self-pity, this song was playing louder and deeper than normal. Then I noticed the back door was slightly ajar.

I rarely used that door, which led to the back alley and the building's trash bins. As a single man who ate out almost every night, my trash generation had been reduced to junk mail and empty beer bottles. As such, my trips to the bins were infrequent. When I did make the occasional trip I most certainly locked the door after I came back. Although I'd grown to like my new neighborhood, I wasn't so much in love to forget it was still a fairly dangerous part of town.

I stared at the thin sliver of black between the door and the frame and never felt so vulnerable to the night as I did at that moment. I took rapid, shortened breaths that felt like pure oxygen. My senses were on overload. The music thumped painfully in my ears, the chill of the bottle numbed my fingers, and the smells of ammonia from the kitchen and fried tortillas from the taquería on the corner made a sickening concoction that tickled high up in my throat.

> *I hoped and I pray that someday*
> *I'll be the vision of your hap-happiness…*

Two fat fingers slipped around the jam and gently pushed the door open. I didn't move. The thought to run never entered my mind. Even the instinctual need for a weapon, any weapon, never surfaced. A small knife was at an arm's length from where I was, yet it remained in the drawer. I just stood there and watched. I watched the door inch open a third of the way and a pale, dead-looking face appeared, partly in shadow from the shaft of light thrown off by the overhead fixture. He stared at me with no emotion. It felt like an hour.

"What are you doing here?" I asked.

The question shook him out of his daze, as if my voice reminded him of why he was there. He pushed the door all the way open, revealing two more men behind him. They were all in leather or dark shirts. They all had their heads shaved. I recognized one of them from the tire shop.

I was transfixed by the sheer terror of strangers entering a space they had no right to be in. I think I hunched over, because I clearly remembered seeing their shoes, even knowing how many laces there were. They came at me in a slow, powerful wave. I held out my arms to defend myself but was immediately thrown back against the refrigerator. I rained harmless blows on the back of one of the attackers. One of his partners easily corralled my arm and pinned it behind me. All three then stepped back, and I was surrounded in a tight half circle. The man with the dead eyes poked at me with his left hand as his right fist came arching in from the side.

I actually leaned in as his fist came crashing against my ear. A warm rush enveloped my body like being submerged in melted wax. I was still on my feet, though slightly hunched over. I reached out to my attackers with a gesture you use when looking for help getting back to your feet. They instead landed punch after punch on my head and neck. My legs felt like rubber bands and only the countertop held me upright. I felt my hair being tugged and then my face hit the linoleum floor. The kicking began, targeting my stomach, legs, and groin.

I entered a state between consciousness and unconsciousness in which I no longer felt the blows but still heard them—that fleshy sound made by blunt trauma on the human body. The initial fear of seeing these men enter the kitchen quickly dissipated, and I slipped into a perverse satisfaction at the thought of getting my ass handed to me. After over twenty years of fending off passive aggression, I was finally faced with the physical kind. And I was taking it.

These bastards could kick me all night if they wanted to, and although I knew the real pain would come later, in that moment, curled up as I was on the linoleum floor, I actually felt great.

The light hurt the most. I had managed to roll onto my back but couldn't find the will to roll back to my side, where the pain hurt less and where the overhead fixture didn't feel like those lamps at the dentist's office. I draped my arm across my face and buried my eyes into the dark, soothing crook under the elbow. I lay there and listened to the labored breathing coming out of my lungs, which had its own lullaby effect. I counted the circles of light that danced on the inside of my eyelids. Just when I thought I had them all counted, they jumbled up and more were added and I had to start counting all over again.

"Jesus!" I heard a voice and then felt a pair of hands on me, this time to comfort, not to harm. They pulled back the arm covering my eyes. "Oh my God," Cheli whispered at what must have been a frightening sight.

That damn light bore down into my head again. I tried to close my eyes but they were already narrowed to slits from the swelling.

"Can you shut off the light? It hurts my eyes," I mumbled.

Cheli ignored me and took out her phone and started dialing.

"What are you doing?"

"Getting you an ambulance."

"No," I said. "I'm fine."

And then to prove it I somehow mustered the strength to pull myself to a seated position against the refrigerator. I slumped there with a hangdog look.

"See."

Cheli reluctantly hung up the phone and sat on the floor next to me.

"You're a mess."

"Yup."

"I told you to not get involved—"

I waved her off.

"No lectures. Please."

I stared at the back door wide open to the night.

"I'm cold," I said.

Cheli pulled at my arms.

"We're going to the emergency room. If you don't help me I will drag you there."

"No," I pleaded. "I don't need to go to the emergency room. I want a hot shower," I said with my head leaning against the refrigerator. "But I don't think I can get there myself."

Cheli dragged me to my feet, and I put most of my weight on her shoulder. I surmised my ribs were cracked from the pain every move and each breath caused. It felt like a ten-mile hike just to get to the bathroom. Cheli gently sat me down on the toilet, took off my shoes and socks, and ran the water in the tub. She helped me off with my shirt.

"Forget the pants," I said, "just help me into the tub."

I gingerly stepped into the tub and the first wave of hot water made me woozy and instantly tired. I didn't think I had the strength to stand so I sat down in the tub and let the water rain down on me.

"Hotter, please," I asked.

Cheli adjusted the temperature. "How does that feel?"

"It stings."

When the boiler ran out of hot water, Cheli helped me back to my feet. I toweled off in the room clouded over with steam. She brought in a change of clothes and helped me get dressed. She led me to the bedroom and gently lowered me onto the mattress. I protested but was asleep before I could even finish the sentence.

The music woke me up some time later. My neighbor was in a groove and deep into his collection of the slow and sad ones. I pulled myself upright and saw Cheli sitting by the window on a chair she had dragged in from the living room.

"My father used to play this song," Cheli remarked. She had that expression of someone who had spent the last hour catching up with an old friend. She looked vulnerable and pretty.

"I never figured Latinos to be oldies fans."

"Didn't you know? Cholos like doo-wop. They get their girl and their beer and slow dance and reminisce about the old days. We Mexicans are a sentimental group."

I watched Cheli drift off as the song came to its sad conclusion. There was a short pause and then it started all over again.

"Want to reminisce with me?" I asked and awkwardly got to my feet. I held out my arms.

"I think you should lie back down. You don't look so good."

"It hurts no matter what," I explained. "It hurts to sit and it hurts to stand. And if that's the case I might as well stand."

"Okay," she said and came to the center of the room. "I'll teach you the cholo dance. Don't worry, it doesn't involve much moving."

The cholo dance was a gentle rocking side to side with both arms pressed against my chest. "You have to point your thumbs up," Cheli instructed. Once I was in the correct position, she wrapped her arms around my waist and rested her cheek on my shoulder. I was a little weak in the legs and leaned heavily on her. Cheli held me up with her arms. "Too tight?" she asked.

"No, it feels good."

We stayed like that for three or four songs. I was dead tired but didn't want it to stop. Eventually my neighbor gave up. He reached his limit and the endless loop gave way to the city sounds that were there all along and only resurfaced once the music stopped.

I pulled back a little to see Cheli's face. Her eyes were swollen with tears. I didn't know how long she had been crying but it appeared to have been for a while. She tried to bury her face in my chest, but I gently pulled her back up and kissed her on the cheek and tasted her tears. I kissed both her eyes and then her lips and held her as tightly as my body would allow.

THE ARROYO

I called in sick the entire week, partly to recover and partly to avoid all the questions about why my face looked like old hamburger meat. The pain got progressively worse with each day until about day three post-beating, when it hurt even if I stood still. I couldn't read, because turning the page of a book required too much energy. I watched a lot of broadcast TV. It's a good thing the network comedies weren't funny, because it hurt too much to laugh.

Mike and I spread the printouts of Claire's emails and pored over them for the better part of a morning. Mike logged each little detail on a legal pad, which by the end was a manic scribble of names, arrows, and underlines. When he was finished he looked down at his work and tapped the big, bold letters that spelled "ARROYO." Without looking me in the eyes he said, "Nice work, Chuck."

For a man with few nice things to say about anyone, those words meant a lot to me.

"Thanks," I said a little too eagerly, for he immediately

reverted to his old self.

"Don't go crowning your ass just yet. This is good information, well earned by the looks of your face, but it's just a piece. A good piece, but a piece all the same."

"Sure," I said.

"It's coming together," he announced. "I knew a cop, an actual honest one, if you can believe that, who used to tell me that the answer to any puzzle is always right in front of you. Everyone else is overly concerned with what's missing. They waste hours trying to track down those bits that got lost from the box. What they don't realize, he told me, is you don't need them to see the big picture. He was a smart man"—and I knew he was talking about his father—"so we got the pieces. Now we have to put them together."

"We have the name of the development, whatever it is going to be—an office building, a mall, a planned community—but we don't really know where it will be built."

"From your wife's emails with McIntyre it seems they're having zoning issues in Lincoln Heights, so we can assume it's going in somewhere around there. It's a shitty place to put in a mall, but what do I know."

"We have a women's center in the same area developed by Carmen Hernandez and paid for by the city via Councilman Abramian. I wonder if that's where Valenti's project is going."

"People bend the rules in this city when it comes to development money," said Mike, "but that seems a stretch to think Valenti could get this building under the guise of women's center and then turn around and make one of his concept malls out of it. Though, remember what he did in Irvine when he got the city to donate some land as part of a wetlands conservation project and then turned around and built condos?

"The other big piece is this block of run-down buildings sold to that person named Salas," he continued. "The sales of these buildings were helped along by the thug Temekian."

"Who sent his boys over to push my face in."

"Did they say anything to you?"

"I couldn't hear anything over the punches."

Mike leaned back and studied the ceiling like there was an answer scrawled along it. "Nothing fits. It feels like it should but it doesn't. Valenti is too big to be playing around with this small-time crook Temekian. And Carmen's history of questionable dealings has never included the rough stuff before, so it's unlikely she's behind it."

"What about that guy who bought the block of buildings on Holcomb Street?"

"I put a full afternoon on that," Mike replied bitterly. "Found nothing. Like he doesn't exist."

"Can you do that?"

"Do what?"

"Buy property under a false name. Or a fake one?"

"Since 9/11 they've cut down on the shenanigans. It used to be you could forge anyone's name on a document, but now everything is aboveboard. I don't see how he could do it, no matter how good Valenti is."

"They must have a Social Security number to file a return. Maybe if you—"

"Don't tell me what I should do," he bristled. "I'll find the bastard." And to fully put me in my place, he added, "How do Langford and your new girlfriend's ex-husband fit in this?" Mike picked up on my look. "Yes, Chuck, I did some research on your lady friend."

"You don't trust anyone, do you?"

"Not really. How much do you know about him?"

"Only that he's dead and he used to do business with Langford."

"He went by the name Don even though his given name was something like Hector," Mike said. "These guys all think changing their name to something Anglo will make them more money." He laughed and then, to prove just how little he trusted people, he laid out a very detailed dossier of Cheli's deceased husband.

Don started as a real estate agent out in San Bernardino County in the early part of the decade. He worked for one of the big firms, but eventually got tired of sharing his commissions, so he got his broker's license and opened his own shop. Everyone was flipping houses like they were trading cards. They'd use the money from a sale to buy more property, leverage it up with loans, do a shitty remodel and sell it for a $150,000 profit. The money was so easy that there were always buyers. The more successful Don got, the farther west he moved.

He outgrew San Berdoo and gradually worked his way toward LA. He and Cheli rode that wave into a four-bedroom palazzo on a Los Feliz hillside. Everyone thought that wave would go on forever.

It's different this time, they used to say.

"It's never different," Mike corrected.

One day everything worked, and then suddenly it stopped. And Don found himself, like most of those guys when the market crashed,, too far out on the branch. Easy money and irrational exuberance are synonymous in the financial thesaurus.

"What happened to him?" I asked.

"He lost everything—all his properties, all his homes, all his rentals, all his parents' money, all his cousins' money, all anyone who ever was foolish enough to invest with him's money. He declared bankruptcy, moved out of their home into a studio apartment in Echo Park, got all his affairs in order, and then shot himself."

I recalled an early conversation with Cheli when she had bitterly told me that Ed took the easy way out with suicide. She might well have been talking about her husband.

"Remember what my father said—all the pieces are right in front of you. You just have to put them together." Mike looked me in the eye. "Chuck, I'll ask that next time you have a piece of the puzzle, you don't withhold from me."

"None of this sounds relevant."

"Probably not, but the rule still applies."

I was sufficiently chastened, but Mike wasn't finished.

"How was she?" he asked as he gathered up his papers.

Although nothing had happened between Cheli and me, I didn't appreciate the question.

"Is that part of the puzzle, too?"

"No, that's just me checking in on a friend."

Mike headed out the door my attackers had used to enter the apartment. He rubbed his hand on the casement they had jimmied open.

"Did you ever ask yourself how those thugs knew you lived here?"

I hadn't. There were only a handful of people who

knew the location of my apartment: Mike and Claire, Cheli, of course, maybe Paul Darbin if he snooped in my personnel file, and one other person.

Rafi got a lot of enjoyment watching me wince as I stood up to shake his hand.

"I'm glad you find my suffering amusing," I told him.

"What does the other guy look like?"

"Three other guys. And not a scratch on them unless you count the nicks they might have gotten on their knuckles as they pounded on me."

"So you think Temekian did this?"

"I recognized one of his AP thugs."

"How do you know they were Armenian?"

I shot him a look.

"Did you tell anyone where I was living?" I asked.

When I originally shared my contact information with Rafi, my current address came over with the phone number in the text. He was one of the few people who had it.

"Either inadvertently or not," I added.

Rafi registered the implication in the last statement, and he didn't like it.

"I haven't seen him in weeks," he answered tersely, "and I never gave no one your stupid address."

I let the din of the coffee shop fill the silence between us.

"Do you think they killed my father?" he asked, his face emotionless and unreadable.

Throughout all the running around and the events that kicked off when Ed disappeared, I'd lost track of the basic tragedy in the situation: that there was a boy still struggling to figure out what happened to his father.

"I don't know," I replied.

"That company that you and my dad work for, they do any kind of lawyer work?" he asked. I was amazed at how little he knew about his father and his line of work, though I had heard similar things with friends who were parents—your kids care about you up until around age eleven; then they stop and don't pick it back up until their mid-twenties.

"Well, we have lawyers on staff, but we aren't a law firm. Why do you ask?"

"Nothing, was just curious."

"It has to be something important or you wouldn't have asked. Do you need legal help?"

"I don't know," he said. "Maybe."

"Did you get into trouble with the police?"

"Just because I'm Armenian doesn't mean I'm a gangster."

"Stop playing the martyr. You know that's not what I meant."

He waited a while before continuing. "I think my grandfather is taking my dad's money."

"How do you know this?"

"He's writing checks using my father's money," Rafi explained. He sounded contrite despite the fact that he hadn't done anything wrong.

"Does your grandfather have authority to draw off your father's accounts?"

"I don't think so. He met with some guy the other day at my uncle's house. I listened in from the kitchen.

They were talking about that one building, the one down in Lincoln Heights."

"The Deakins?"

"Yeah. They were trying to figure out a way to sell it without my dad's approval. This guy sounded like some kind of expert. He said there were ways around it, that my dad didn't actually have to sign over the documents."

"Can you describe this man?" I asked.

Rafi gave me a description that fit the man I had spoken to from GVK Properties, the man whose name I could never remember.

"I am going to talk to your grandfather."

"Please don't say anything. This is a family thing," he said. I knew he meant something among Armenians that needed to be settled among Armenians.

"Well, I know some lawyers, but none of them are Armenian."

"That's okay. For that I want a white guy," he said, laughing. "Will this lawyer need money? I mean, how much will it cost?"

"Pro bono," I lied. "They'll work for free as a favor to me."

If I had told him that I would pay for their services, he would never have contacted them. He had a lot of pride for such a young man. We chatted a bit more, commenting on all the fancy cars parked in the lot and the fact that no one seemed to have a job that required they spend the better part of the afternoon in an office.

"This is their office," he explained.

As I got up to leave, Rafi called out to me.

"Hey. I never told him where you lived."

"I know you didn't, Rafi."

"If it means anything," he said, "Temekian usually hangs out at the bakery on the corner of Geneva and Harvard. Though I wouldn't go strolling in there unless you want your face pushed in again."

I didn't have to worry about that. By the time I arrived at the bakery the entire block had been cordoned off by the Glendale PD. All attention was on a nondescript storefront where the gaggle of police officers parted ways to let Cheli lead a handcuffed Ardavan Temekian to a waiting cruiser.

WHAT'S IN A ZONE?

I t's a prescription drug scam. Temekian's crew picks up homeless guys, usually vets, and drives them around to a handful of shady Armenian doctors in East Hollywood who write out prescriptions, usually for oxycodone. In one day the guy can collect up to ten prescriptions. Temekian pays off his runner and sells the pills on the street for around twenty bucks a pop."

We sat in my living room and ate noodles that Cheli had grabbed in Chinatown on the way to my apartment. She tried to play it cool, but her excitement came through the pitch of her voice.

"I've been on this one for seven months. We picked up one of the doctors on a statutory rape charge and got him to turn on Temekian. The man was pissed off when I told him how much those pills sold for. I guess he wasn't getting paid that much."

She sort of smiled to herself, the same look she had when I saw her leading Temekian to the police cruiser. While her male counterparts watched her with a mixture of admiration and envy, I felt only the first part.

"What?" she asked, suddenly shy under my gaze.

"I'm happy for you," I said.

She laughed nervously and waved it off, shifting the attention away from her.

"So, what'd you guys find out?"

I filled her in on what Mike and I had pieced together from Claire's emails on the Arroyo. There were also the bits I'd learned from Rafi and the current attempts to sell the Deakins Building. And finally, there was what little we'd learned about the mysterious figure Salas who was behind the purchase of several buildings on Holcomb. I hoped for a similar reaction to the one I had a moment ago, but Cheli simply listened and grew more sullen the more I spoke.

"Everything okay?" I finally asked.

That seemed to bring her out of her daze.

"Chuck, I'm sorry I've been sort of disconnected for a while."

Truth was I hadn't heard a word from her since the night I got beat up in my apartment, despite several attempts to reach her. I was hesitant to admit it, both to Cheli and to myself, just how disappointing that was. What began as an attraction more toward the job that came with the woman was quickly becoming an attraction to the woman herself. And I wasn't sure I was ready for it.

"Sounds like you've been busy," I said, giving us both an easy out.

She didn't take it.

"It has nothing to do with work. I've been distant for a reason."

"Okay."

"It's a weird time for me. I haven't really been with anyone since my husband passed. Maybe I'm a little afraid, a little guarded, a little…I don't know what."

"That's understandable."

"But not fair," she said. "It's not fair to you. I have a bunch going on in my head. Maybe just go easy on me, okay?"

"I don't even know what that means," I said.

"Me either."

I took her hand and we sat in an awkward, antici-patory silence.

"Where's your neighbor and the music?"

"It must be his night off."

We kissed in the quiet and slowly got comfortable with each other and put away whatever thoughts of failed marriages and past loves still lingered. Cheli spent the night and even part of the morning. Maybe it was the awkwardness of the evening or even the Spartan set-ting with the mattress on the floor, but the whole thing felt like a college romance betweeen adults.

"I got jobs to run," Rosie said as I approached. She had her boots propped up on the coffee table in our recep-tion area, much to the annoyance of the woman man-ning the front desk. She also kept her call radio at a volume set for traffic noise and not the hushed tones of my office.

"Here's your package," she said, but as I grabbed the padded envelope, she held tightly onto her end. With raised eyebrows she asked, "Aren't you forgetting something?"

I looked around nervously. The receptionist wasn't watching us, but I could tell she had her ear trained in our direction.

"Will you take a check?" I asked.

Rosie's blank stare was my answer to that.

We went downstairs to the building lobby so I could get money out of the ATM. Rosie pocketed the cash and handed me the package. It was heavy.

"Give me a minute to run up and make a copy," I said.

"I already did," Rosie answered. "One for you and one for me in case any of this comes back to bite me in the ass."

Rosie collected her bike, which she had left leaning against the security desk. The guard looked up from his monitors. "You know, Miss," he said, "you can't have your bike on the premises."

I always wondered if part of the training for building security was to learn unnecessary vocabulary like "vacate" and "visual reconnaissance." Before I could "assuage" the man's concern, Rosie resolved it her way.

"Fuck off," she said and rode her bike out of the building. "I'll call you if anything else comes through," she shouted to me.

Back in my office, I spread the contents of the package out on the table. It was a series of documents from the City of Los Angeles, Department of City Planning. On a note stuck to one of the papers, I recognized Claire's writing, it said: "Final presentation for the Wed meeting."

They were mainly legal documents with enough jargon and legalese to make it read like a foreign language.

Where the security guards had "premises," the lawyers had "pursuant." It must have made them both feel special to be a part of a club that had its own language. Near the back of all this nonsense was something that caught my eye.

It was a map of eastern LA crisscrossed with a dizzying array of shapes and colors that resembled a Jackson Pollock painting. The colors represented the various zones, sub-zones, overlay zones, and whatever-kind-of zones that carved up the city. It looked like the plan of a schizophrenic: the result of decades' worth of wrangling, manipulation, special-interest lobbying, compromise, and bribery—the bastard child of a city conceived over a lust for land. And it was all about to change.

Directly behind this map was a second one of the same area, only with some tweaks to the zones. Apparently Zone 8 was being revised. The original Zone 8 stretched from the upper-middle-class neighborhood of South Pasadena into parts of Highland Park. The proposed additions were two streams that dribbled south off the hills of Montecito Heights down into Lincoln Heights where, by the time they ended, they were no more than a block wide.

I didn't have to research the significance of this change, because it was already abundantly clear—the revised zone would now include Carmen's women's center, the Deakins Building, and the forced-sale homes on Holcolm Street.

There was some good old-fashioned gerrymandering going on between Claire and McIntyre. I assumed the manipulation of zones had to benefit Valenti's project, the Arroyo.

I did a quick internet search on the Area Planning Commission proposing these changes. Timothy Carlson had once been employed by the mega-contractor Simons & Siefort, which along with Valenti's firm had developed much of the former farmland in Irvine. Valenti eventually absorbed Simons & Siefort, but it was unclear if Carlson had made the transition with the purchase. At various points in his career, he'd sat on several corporate boards, including Signature Homes, one of the phone numbers Ed had called from the Resting Room. A quick search revealed that Signature Homes was the real estate division of Valenti's concept malls and fell under the group McIntyre controlled. The office addresses of Signature Homes and Valenti's operation were identical.

"Starting to feel a little incestuous," I said to Mike. I heard him chuckle on the other end of the phone.

"Cast a light on the power structure that shapes this city and you quickly realize it's a small, tight-knit group with few rotating members," he explained. "It lets you get things done within the bureaucracy. The great flaw, however, is the same one that plagued the royal families—when you exclude new blood from entering your circle you end up having to fuck your sister."

"Then we need to figure out who's screwing whom."

"Follow the money," Mike said. "Area Planning Commissions operate off an ever-shrinking, taxpayer-funded budget and an ever-growing pool of development fees paid for by the mega-contractors. It's also an appointed position," he added.

"By whom?"

"Better to ask who confirms them," he corrected.

A LESSON IN CIVIC DUTY

City Hall was a large, white obelisk that once stood as the tallest structure in Los Angeles—that is, until engineers figured out how to build fifty-story steel-and-glass structures on rollers. These towering marvels could withstand the rocking and rolling of an 8.0 earthquake. They were the symbols of the new downtown, but that didn't mean the city catered to them. City Hall may have been surpassed in height, but the institutional power of this town would forever be contained within its walls.

The public entrance led into a dimly lit lobby with stone floors whose patina could only come from decades of floor wax and weekly polishing. Original wall sconces and colored shades cast the area in a cathedral-like hue that, when paired with the subtle echoes from the coffered ceiling, gave you a sense of urgency to find a seat before Mass started.

I made my way to the creaky elevators and the fifth floor, where the public hearing was being held for the requested zone changes. It was your typical municipal government forum. The room could hold a hundred people, but only the official participants and their administrators actually showed. That didn't stop them from using microphones to speak to each other even though the entire group sat within a twenty-foot radius.

"Sit anywhere?" I asked the security guard stationed at the door.

He looked at me and then the empty rows of chairs and then back to me. He didn't have the energy to give a verbal response.

"I guess you aren't expecting a big turnout," I joked and headed for a seat.

As I chose my chair in the last row, I realized I was being watched intently by the seven committee members at the dais. They seemed perplexed that someone from the public would actually attend a public forum. Or it could have been that my badly bruised face hinted that a deranged, rather than a civic-minded, individual was in attendance.

The agenda was long and convoluted and read aloud by an overweight technocrat in a rumpled suit who had a voice that could cure insomnia. The zone change was somewhere near the end of the list of things they had to discuss, so I had to endure a full hour of motions, seconds, and approvals.

The technocrat was a special breed of middle-class American quite distinct from his corporate cousins. Both were sentenced to a life's work of quiet oblivion, but where the corporate cogs fabricated their relevance through mission statements and anniversary milestones, the bureaucrat resigned himself to an existence of little consequence and instead focused all of his efforts on accruing tenure so as to retire with maximum benefits.

"Item 752B," announced the clerk, "proposed revision of municipal code as pertains to division 621, Zone 8."

I jolted upright as the blood coursed back through my body. The technocrat had somehow managed to lull me into a deep REM sleep. I scanned the room. There were two new people in attendance. The first sat at the conference table before the dais. He wore a casual blazer that looked expensive, an open-collared shirt, and smart, tortoise-framed glasses. It was a look that only the very young or the very wealthy could pull off. Even the overhead fluorescent lights couldn't wash out that wonderfully golden tan that one got from yachting or playing tennis.

The other person who had joined the hearing was Claire. We caught eyes and acknowledged each other through a look. Or, more accurately, I stared and she just glared.

"Mr. Carlson?" the clerk announced to the gentleman at the conference table. It was his signal to speak. As Carlson read through his motion, I got the sense that he didn't understand the language or grasped its content. One of the committee members even had to correct him a few times. At one point the clerk asked if there were any objections to the requested revision. I found myself being stared down by all seven members of the committee. Carlson slowly turned in my direction as well. Claire trained her eyes on the floor as if praying that I wouldn't speak.

But I felt the need to say something. Exactly what I should say was a mystery. I gingerly made my way forward to the microphone set up in the aisle.

"Hello?" I said, tapping the microphone to see if it was on.

"Go ahead, sir," instructed one of the committee members. "State your name and occupation, please."

"Charles Restic, human resources manager," I said and watched as Carlson wrote down my name.

"Did you have a comment?" asked another committee member. They appeared increasingly annoyed by my presence.

"I do," I said.

"The floor is yours."

"Can I ask a question to Mr. Carlson?"

"You will address all comments to the committee and the committee will determine whether to pursue any further questioning of Mr. Carlson."

"Well, that doesn't make much sense," I muttered, not entirely meaning to say it out loud.

"Mr. Restic, we ask that you respect the time of everyone in this room and please get on with your comments."

"Okay, fine," I said. "I believe there are improprieties involved with this zone change that you should be aware of." I rattled off all the details Mike and I had discovered in as coherent a fashion as I could, having been put on the spot on such short notice. During my five-minute-plus speech, not a single committee member took notes. When I finished, all six members at the dais stared at me and said nothing. We remained in that uncomfortable silence for nearly half a minute until one of the members finally spoke up.

"Are you finished?" he asked.

"Well, did you understand what I just laid out?"

"We did," he remarked. "Have you concluded your remarks?"

"I, I don't know. Are there any questions?"

"There are none. Have you concluded your remarks?" he repeated.

All eyes in the room willed me to state that I had finished. There seemed to be no debate over what I had said, but also no real acknowledgment of the facts I had brought to their attention. It was an unsatisfying conclusion. Just as I was about to confirm that I was done, the tired voice of the security guard a few feet from me whispered, "Request a formal review."

I looked over at him. He still appeared half-asleep and stared dully at some spot on the far wall. I don't think anyone else in the room heard him. I leaned back into the microphone. "I'd like to request a formal review of the proposed change."

Apparently my somnolent friend was a bit of an expert on procedural rule, because those simple words sent the committee into a tizzy. I believe I heard Claire curse me out from across the room.

"Could you please repeat that?" asked one of the committee members, but the woman to his right cut him off.

"What are you making him repeat it for? We all heard it," she said.

The clerk took the councilwoman's lead, and pronounced a deferment of approval on the proposed change until a formal review of the revision was completed.

"Wait," said a befuddled Carlson. "What happened?"

"By rule, we must conduct a review by an

independent party."

"Well, how long is that going to take?" he asked.

"Sixty days."

※   ※   ※

"You're acting like a child," Claire remarked as we made our way through the lobby and around the security check-point. She seemed to finally notice the extent of the damage on my face but then used it as further proof of my adolescent behavior. "You're getting into fights now, too?"

"I got this by asking too many questions," I replied. "But if exposing the truth is deemed childish, then I am happy to take up the mantle."

"Come down off the cross. We need the wood."

"That's Mike's line."

She stopped and stared me down. "Now it all makes sense."

"What does?"

"Why you're making an ass of yourself in public forums and generally acting like an overall nuisance. Is this Mike's doing?"

"No."

"It sure smells like him."

Her tone was grating. She reverted into lawyer mode. "What is your interest in the Arroyo?"

"Stop speaking to me like it's a deposition. And you know why I am interested. Because it's connected to Ed's disappearance."

"There's no proof of that."

"Come off it, you know there is. And the more you play dumb, the stronger the connection gets. Did you architect the zone change?"

"I would choose another word to describe it, but we did have input on the final decision."

"Why?"

She paused. "It would be beneficial to our client. And it's perfectly legal. We would never knowingly put our client in any risk of future legal complications."

"What about Langford? Have you ever worked with him before?"

"You know I have," she said.

"On the Deakins Building?"

Another pause. "Yes."

"Do you know Ardavan Temekian?"

"No."

"Are you involved in any deals with properties on Holcomb Street?"

"Where? No, I don't know those properties," she said. "Now who's making this out to be a deposition?"

"How well do you know McIntyre?" I asked.

"Why?" she asked warily.

"Come on, Claire, I'm not an idiot. I know about you two. But how well do you know him?"

"You have no right to ask me these things."

"These guys are not kids. They play a grown-up game, and they play rough. Look at what happened to Ed. To Langford. Look at my face! Three thugs broke into my home and beat the living shit out of me the other night. Because I'm finding stuff out that someone doesn't want me to. And you see how they handle those situations. Don't get yourself wrapped up in something you will later regret."

"Todd doesn't have anything to do with…with that murder. With whoever attacked you."

"Glad to see you and Todd know each other so well that you can read each other's thoughts."

"Screw you, Chuck."

"Don't say I didn't warn you."

Claire suddenly got very aloof. "Apparently you can't accept this marriage ending."

"What the hell does that mean?" I shot back.

"Why else are you running around doing everything in your power to annoy me? I've moved on, Chuck. And none of this is going to change that." Like a good defense attorney, she stopped speaking when she knew she was ahead.

But Claire was Claire, and she couldn't resist the urge to pile on. "One more thing," she said by the exit. "Break into my house again and you're going to get your ass bitten off by a Doberman."

THE AQUARIUM ON THE HILL

The black sedan with just its parking lights on idled in front of my apartment. I walked up to the passenger door, but the driver never got out. I was forced to knock on the window.

"Are you here for me?" I asked as the window rolled down.

The driver was an elderly Latino man with dyed hair slicked straight back. He wore the standard attire, a starched white shirt and black pants. The interior of the car smelled like vanilla air freshener.

"Are you Mr. Restic?" he asked me.

"I am."

"Then I am here for you."

He made no move to open the door for me. Neither did he give any indication of where I was supposed to sit. Since I have a natural discomfort with the vestiges of hierarchy and a class system, I sat in the front seat. It was clearly the wrong choice.

"You're welcome to sit in the back," he offered.

I got the call that Valenti wanted to meet me the night after the incident at the public hearing. Mike and

Cheli were with me in my apartment when the unregistered number came up on my cell. I assumed Claire had given my number to her client. We were recapping an eventful day that had Easy Mike placing calls to all the participants in this drama with the hope of getting quotes for his soon-to-be-published article. Everyone stuck to the script. Carmen Hernandez fell back on "necessary care for the underserved." For McIntyre, it was all about "job creation," and Councilman Abramian spouted off concerns about "the dangers of high-density projects." When the call came, the young woman didn't ask me to meet as much as she instructed me when the car would arrive to pick me up.

"I've been summoned," I told them. "Anyone want to join me?"

Mike declined. He had a lead on the buyer of the properties on Holcomb—the elusive Salas. Cheli had to meet with the assistant district attorney over Temekian's upcoming arraignment.

"I guess I'm going solo then."

We caught a light on Griffin and were forced to wait at the intersection. At this time of night there was little traffic and even fewer pedestrians. A homeless man with a shopping cart full of mementos crossed in front of our car. He paused in the headlights to stare at us. His gaze went from the driver to me and then back to the driver.

"I give up, officers!" he shouted.

The driver scowled and hit the accelerator, sweeping his sedan dangerously close to the shopping cart. He ran two more red lights before we reached the freeway.

"How long have you worked for Mr. Valenti?"

"A long time," he said.

"You must have seen a lot."

"I haven't seen nothing," he replied curtly.

"What's Mr. Valenti like?" I probed further.

His silence clearly indicated there would be no more idle chitchat. We drove the rest of the way in silence. We glided across the flats of Los Angeles to the Westside, where we took the 405 North a few exits and then fell into the tree-lined streets of Bel-Air and then Beverly Hills. From there we worked our way up to the top of Benedict Canyon and Mulholland Drive.

The driver instinctively guided us along the dark and winding road. It felt like he could do this drive with his eyes closed. We eventually took a cutoff that was all but invisible from the street. This led to a large gate that opened automatically as the sedan approached. A uniformed man stood watch in a small, well-lit structure nearby. We tracked a narrow driveway lined with looming cypress trees that stood like tin soldiers in silhouette against the night sky. Then the house appeared before us.

It was a massive structure of glass and stone and undulating waves of polished steel that represented all that was wrong with form over function. Two-ton steel girders muscled into twisted shapes jutted out over the canyon and served no other purpose than the aesthetic. Every section had dedicated accent lights. The spectacle would make Hollywood cinematographers blush.

I found myself in awe more at the volume of material that went into the building than of the building itself. It was as if they encased the entire structure in burnished steel for no other reason than "because I can."

I waited for instructions but received none.

"Good talking to you," I said as I got out of the car and headed toward the main entrance.

I took the few steps up to the twelve-foot door that was either teak or mahogany and most certainly expensive. Through its glass panel, I saw a young woman patiently waiting in a cushioned chair in the foyer. Before I could ring the bell, she sprang to her feet and hefted the giant door open. She wore a tight-fitting sweater and pencil skirt. She had cold blue eyes and such perfectly white teeth that they almost looked fake. In business, your brand is determined by how others perceive you. Placing this little minx at the front door sent a clear message—Valenti ran an elegant, sophisticated operation that could rip your face off with a single swipe.

"Welcome, Mr. Restic," she purred and led me into a large room just off the foyer. "Can I get you a sparkling mineral water, cappuccino?"

"Do you have any organic soda?" I asked, if for no other reason than to be an ass in the face of pretense.

"Mango or blackberry?" she countered.

"Strawberry?" I tried again.

"I'm afraid we ran out," she replied.

"Thank you," I said, sounding disappointed. "But I think I will pass."

"Very well," she replied and drifted out of the room.

I looked around the impressive space. The entire far wall was a floor-to-ceiling window, an expansive sheet of non-reflective glass that gave the illusion that you were out in the open air. I drifted over like a leaf in a slow-moving stream. The entire city of Los Angeles lay at my feet—from the garish lights of the Ferris wheel on the Santa Monica Pier, to the grid work of suburban dreams across the great plain of the city, to the lighted matchsticks of the downtown skyscrapers winking in the far distance.

"Nice of you to come, Chuck," said a smiling McIntyre, who strode across the room to greet me. He squeezed my hand just to the point of the knuckles cracking and held it a quarter-second too long to make it feel genuine. He had the confidence of a man who could stare another in the eyes for a prolonged period and feel no awkwardness.

Todd McIntyre fit the part of the real estate development executive down to the open-collar shirt and navy blazer they all seemed to wear. I checked to see if he was wearing socks with his loafers. Easy Mike often said that all men named Todd were jerk-offs, and he'd defy you to think of an exception. Few won that game. It was as if simply selecting that name for your baby predestined him to a life as a manipulative, whiny, self-serving brat.

"I wish we could meet under better circumstances," he said plaintively, "but I thought it was important to get together and maybe talk over some of the issues between us." He spoke like we were rival haberdashery owners about to discuss a price war on derbies that was hurting both our businesses.

"Where's Mr. Valenti?"

"He's on a call with Asia and will be joining us shortly."

"Well, which *issue* should we start with? The business related or the personal?" Despite my attempt to remain calm, I was already introducing tension into the conversation.

"Let's start with the professional," he said with a clipped laugh.

"So you want to know why I objected to the proposed zone change."

"Do you have any legitimate concerns with the proposal?"

"Define 'legitimate.'"

McIntyre let that one pass without commenting.

"If legitimate means seeing that a power broker with his fingers in the city's candy jar doesn't manipulate his way into yet another sweetheart deal, then yes, I do have legitimate concerns about the zone change."

"I'm sorry," he said, "I don't understand. We have done nothing improper in our support—"

"Come off it, McIntyre," I interrupted. "You authored the proposal. Or at least my wife did. You and Valenti are bending people over to get what you want. And that's fine if you want to play these development games with your country club cronies, except this time it's affecting the people down at the bottom, the ones who bring you the clean towel after the squash match." It felt good to play the martyr, and although tempting, I resisted the urge to use the phrase "blood on your hands."

"I don't understand that last reference."

"The Arroyo," I said. He studied me for a few moments. "Are you surprised I know about that?" Again he chose not to respond. "I know more about this project than you probably think." I listed some of the details to prove my point, including the shady dealings around Carmen Hernandez's women's center and the Deakins Building.

"We're not building anything on those properties."

"Then why the zone change that happens to include two thin slivers where all those properties sit?"

"I will reiterate—we are not building anything on those properties."

"Does the name Ed Vadaresian mean anything to you?"

McIntyre studied me like he was formulating the well-calculated response that wouldn't come back to haunt him later.

"I've never met Mr. Vadaresian in person, but we are linked through that property you mentioned, the Deakins Building."

"You know he's been missing for six months?"

"Yes, I heard that."

I decided to gamble.

"And that Mr. Vadaresian called your office the day he disappeared."

"Yes."

That threw me.

"You knew that?"

"I spoke to Mr. Vadaresian."

"What about?"

"I'm afraid I can't discuss that."

"Why not?" I asked. He was growing cagey, and I was growing frustrated with his quick, short responses. He added another.

"It's improper."

"Listen, *Todd*," I said. "This man has been missing, and no one seems to be able or willing to find him. His family is searching for answers and finding none. And then we find out that he called you the day he disappeared, and you aren't willing to discuss the details? Whatever business concern you have pales next to a man's life. Maybe you should reconsider, or I might be forced to involve the authorities in this."

"Mr. Restic?"

I turned to see an elderly man with a shock of white hair approaching. Valenti was smaller than I imagined he would be. When images are formed through photographs in the media, people somehow take on the largeness of their personalities. Without the custom suit and the entourage, he was just an elderly man with a warm smile and gray, watery eyes—someone you'd be happy to have as your grandfather.

"I was just about to explain to Mr. Restic that there is no need to involve the authorities—"

Valenti cut him off with a casual wave.

"Todd, maybe Mr. Restic and I could speak in private."

McIntyre didn't like being dismissed, but he knew better than to challenge his boss. He didn't get into that role by sharing his opinions too often. Once McIntyre had slunk out of the room to join the young minx in the hallway, Valenti turned his attention back to me.

"Thank you for taking the time to meet this late in the evening," he said, motioning me to a set of white couches while he sat in a low-back chair. We sat for a few moments in silence, each man sizing the other up. Valenti came to his conclusion first.

"So this is the man who's cost me money," he said with a tinge of disbelief. For some reason I felt the need to apologize.

"My intention was never to cause you personal loss, Mr. Valenti."

"And what was the intention, then?"

"Find justice for a friend," I answered.

"I didn't know you and Mr. Vadaresian were friends," he replied. McIntyre clearly had done a thorough job of briefing Valenti before our meeting. Men like him always wanted to be the one in the room with the most information. "Plus, I am not sure I see the connection between your friend's disappearance and an insignificant zoning change."

"If it was so insignificant, I don't believe I would be here now."

"Indeed." Valenti shifted in his chair. "Let's be frank with each other, if we may. I've always found that negotiations go a hell of a lot quicker when people are forthright."

"I didn't know we were negotiating."

"Men are always negotiating," he declared. "Let me start, to show my good faith. This is what I know about you. Recently separated from your wife of twelve years, having lost her to a younger and more successful man. Your career path, if charted on a line graph, would resemble a healthy spike twenty years ago and a relatively flat line since then. You have no children, no family in the city, deceased parents. You reluctantly do volunteer work and have no extracurricular obsessions like golf to occupy your free time. You have no real vices on any public record; you're sensible enough with your money to know to buy an air conditioner in winter and Christmas decorations in summer. On the surface you are an upstanding citizen with a full life of relative comfort ahead of you. But underneath you are an incurably bored man, desperately searching for some scrap of validation to paste onto a very respectable but anonymous life."

"Thank you, Doctor," I joked, failing to mask how much the assessment angered me. "How much do I owe you?"

"I'm sorry if this was too blunt. Now, it is your turn," he said and settled deeper into his chair.

"I don't like this game. Plus, I don't know anything about you."

"You must know something. Tell me what you know."

"You're wealthy."

"Obviously."

"Extremely wealthy," I corrected. "The kind of wealth that buys a lot of influence."

"We can debate that. But I will stop interrupting."

"Thank you. You collect art, mostly American and, by the looks of it, mostly ugly. You tend to buy up-and-coming artists and thus create the market for their work. After all, if Valenti owns them they must be worth something. You keep threatening to build a museum with your collection, but it has to be on your terms. There's a pissing contest among the major metropolitan areas for who has the most culture. You exploit this by forcing the city to give you land leases for pennies on the dollar if you promise to let them pay for an elaborate building to house your private collection." This elicited a smile from the old man. "Everything is a business to you, even philanthropy. You don't give money away; you lord it over people. Nothing is free. Even the free money comes with some sort of barter to be collected at a future date. Life to you is one giant, evolving transaction in which two sides negotiate and one comes out on top." I paused for a moment. "That felt good," I said truthfully.

"I told you it would," he confirmed, showing little emotion. "I have one quibble, however, with what was otherwise an accurate summary. Business transactions are not a zero-sum game. You made it sound like there are only winners and losers, but for every deal you make, both parties must gain something. It's simple math. Otherwise you would quickly run out of business partners."

"So who stood to gain by revising the city's zones?"

"A lot of people stand to gain."

"Ed Vadaresian didn't. Bill Langford didn't."

"I can't be held responsible for the actions of people trying to exploit the work we are doing. Let me ask you, would you hold the manufacturer of a butcher knife responsible for murder because a housewife got fed up with her abusive husband?"

"Your analogy doesn't hold water when the people under your employ are involved."

"No one on my staff had anything to do with those murders."

"Who said Ed Vadaresian was murdered?"

Valenti paused. "I assumed some nefarious conclusion to Mr. Vadaresian's disappearance, but you are correct: we cannot be certain he was murdered."

"Why am I even up here?"

"Because you cost me money."

"Whatever I cost you could be recouped by selling one of the lesser-known works of your lesser-known artists."

"You're missing the point that you yourself made about me. It's about the money. I don't like losing money, even if it is a nickel. Why would I keep working like I am? Lord knows I have enough money to keep me living the way I do for decades. Enough money for my daughter and granddaughter to live like this for their entire lives. I like making deals. And this deal is not going as I wanted it to."

"Maybe this deal wasn't meant to be."

That got him to sit up.

"Mr. Restic, how can I persuade you to be more accommodating?"

"Why does that sound like a threat?"

"I didn't make a fortune by threatening people," he said. "I made it by making friends. I like to say, business relationships are like rabbits—they keep breeding new ones."

"You must have quite a warren."

"It's a very productive bunch."

"So you want to be friends," I stated.

"I would enjoy that very much."

"And what does this friendship involve?"

"One place to start is the Arroyo and this whole zoning disagreement. The other is with your acquaintance, Mr. Michael Wagner. I'd prefer he didn't write the article, but if he does, I would ask that he treat us fairly."

"And what do I get?"

"An exit out of your humdrum existence," he answered. "I want you to work for me. You could be very valuable to us, and we in turn could provide equal worth to you."

As he spoke, I felt little pinpricks on the back of my neck and shoulders, and on the tips of my fingers, like the onset of an anxiety attack. I suddenly became very aware of my breathing and could feel my heart beating in my throat. Valenti paused to savor the discomfort his words were having on me. He pressed harder.

"I know you want to break out of this life of yours.

Prove to everyone and to yourself that you're alive. And maybe in the process you win your wife back."

I found myself out of the chair and back in front of the wall of windows. I just wanted out from under that little man's gaze. I didn't want him to see how much his words rattled me. Adjusting to the night outside, my eyes darted from one flicker of light to the next, searching for an anchor to slow this whirlpool of thoughts in my head. I could feel the coldness of the air outside coming through the glass.

"You're on a treadmill, Chuck," intoned the voice behind me. "All you have to do is step off."

Below was the spectacle of a great city, unfolding its collective drama while I watched from the aquarium on the hill. Suspended in this glassed-in room before the immensity of the night crystallized my insignificance. But with this realization came a soothing calm of acceptance.

"I don't want to be your friend, Mr. Valenti," I breathed into the glass.

CINDER BLOCKS

They found the car on a barren street in an industrial area in southeast LA. There was little in the way of pedestrian traffic, as the loft movement hadn't quite reached that section of the city. The only activity came from the huge rigs that moved in and out of the seemingly endless grid of small warehouses. Easy Mike's car stood unnoticed for nearly seventy-two hours, as did his lifeless body hunched over the center console.

I was in the middle of a touch base with one of my direct reports when I got the call. The illusion of associate development was paramount in the corporate world, and as such, these individualized sessions demanded my undivided attention. I let the call go directly to voicemail and listened to it later. Three words into the message, I knew it was bad news.

"It's Terry Ricohr."

The fact that he used his first name meant something was wrong.

"What happened?" I whispered to the blinking red light.

"Mike Wagner has been killed," the voice answered. "Please call me." After a long pause, "I'm sorry."

I drove down to the crime scene and parked in an open slot. I strode past a long line of angry truckers idling at the block's entrance, where two police cars formed a pincer to keep traffic from entering. The off-ramp from the 10 freeway was one block over, and the truckers eagerly awaited the moment when they could dump their loads and head off on the next run.

Detective Ricohr met me at the end of the street and quietly alerted the patrol officers that I was a friend of the deceased. He led me down the street to Mike's car. The driver's side window was down, and even from this distance I could see the spray of black dots that covered the passenger side door.

"We just have a couple of questions for you." Detective Ricohr motioned to another detective, a middle-aged Latino with a bushy mustache and pockmarked cheeks. The man pulled himself from a conversation with a forensics technician and sauntered over. "This is Detective Lopez."

The man nodded and immediately broke into his questioning.

"How long have you known the deceased?"

"Almost ten years."

"What's your relationship?"

"Friends."

"When's the last time you saw the deceased?"

"Wednesday evening. He was at my apartment. He left around four o'clock in the afternoon."

"Do you know where he was heading when he left?"

I explained the lead he'd gotten on the buyer of the

Holcomb Street properties, which then required me to explain all of the details surrounding the investigation that had begun with Ed's disappearance.

"Yes, Detective Ricohr has filled me in on some of this. Where were you between seven and ten in the evening?"

"I was with Carl Valenti at his residence."

The detectives shared a look.

"What were you meeting about?"

"He wanted me and Mike to stop meddling with a project he is working on. Maybe he just wanted to separate us."

"Are you insinuating that Carl Valenti had a hand in this?"

"Insinuating isn't a strong enough word."

"Mr. Restic, have you ever known the deceased to use drugs?"

"Mike? The guy never even took aspirin."

Detective Lopez made a few notes.

"Did he have any enemies that we should know about? He rubbed a lot of people the wrong way in his column."

"He told the truth," I answered.

I detected a snicker from Detective Lopez.

"Is there an issue, Detective?"

"Excuse me?"

"You seemed to laugh just now."

"Did I? I apologize. I meant nothing by it." Detective Lopez didn't seem very sorry. "We just need to follow up on leads that could have led to your friend's murder. Unfortunately, this process can bring out the ugly side of people's lives."

"What ugly side?"

"We all have ugly sides."

"Why don't you enlighten me on Mike Wagner's?" I challenged.

"Mr. Restic, I just deal with what I know, and one of the things I know is that your friend wasn't exactly a popular guy in this town. He wrote a lot of things about a lot of people, and some of the things he wrote people would say weren't accurate. That tends to piss people off. Maybe he pissed off the wrong person."

"Fuck you," I calmly told him.

"Take it easy," Detective Ricohr warned.

"I'm not going to let him throw this bullshit out there."

"I'm only stating the facts," countered Lopez.

"So that's how it goes, huh? You hold some kind of grudge against a man who wrote something you didn't agree with. And now that he's dead it's payback time."

"I'm doing my job, Mr. Restic," Detective Lopez replied icily.

"Sure you are. Probably going to phone it in."

"Listen, I know you're upset," he said.

"Oh, come on. Don't try and take the high road with me, Detective. My friend wasn't perfect, but he did his job well and that's all he was doing. He deserves better."

"Which is exactly what he's going to get. We work equally hard no matter who the deceased is."

In his words was a condemnation—Mike may not have been worthy of the hard work they were going to put into finding his killer but they would do it anyway.

"No wonder everyone hates cops," I muttered under my breath.

Detective Ricohr stepped in and led me off to the side of the street before the confrontation escalated any further.

"Mind if we sit?" he asked. "It's my feet again."

I joined him on the curb. We sat there in silence for a few minutes and watched the proceedings like spectators.

"Nice speech," Ricohr said, breaking the silence. "I'm not sure if you were trying to get them to work harder or get them to blow you off entirely."

"I'm sorry, Detective. I lost my temper. He didn't deserve all the things I said."

"He'll get over it."

"I probably owe him an apology."

Detective Ricohr told me to forget it. "Five years ago," he began, "Detective Lopez and seven men in his precinct were accused of using department resources for weekend benders to Vegas. Not only did they take unauthorized vehicles, they used the sirens to clear the way during patches of traffic. I'm sure I don't need to tell you that hookers were also involved. It all came out in excruciating detail in your friend's column. Detective Lopez got off relatively light, but it did cost him a few years of his retirement. I guess his ass is still a little chapped about it." Detective Ricohr looked around conspiratorially. "Don't tell anyone this, but I was a fan of his column."

"Really?"

"It pissed me off to no end, but it was good."

"That's probably the best compliment anyone could pay him."

Detective Ricohr stretched his legs and then pulled them back in. He rested his forearms on his knees and spoke into the ground.

"The coroner took your friend back downtown. Is there anyone we need to alert? Family?"

I shook my head. "His mom died years ago."

"Was he married?"

"No."

The long silence sank in.

"Do I have to do it?" I asked him.

"It'll make it easier for us if you do."

I looked around at the flat expanse of windowless cinder block and brick buildings, with their loading docks and chain-link fences topped with barbed wire. Every inch of land was entombed in concrete and asphalt, and yet there was an unintentional beauty about it. The lulling rush of the distant freeway traffic was the only sound in the otherwise quiet, still air. It was a very peaceful place at that moment.

"Okay," I said, "let's go."

I had seen death before but had never actually felt the emptiness until my father died. He had been diagnosed with pancreatic cancer three months prior, and his descent was almost immediate. Instead of a long, slow decline, it was like my father fell off a cliff.

We decided his final days should be spent in hospice rather than in the cold, sterile hospital room at Mass General. We set him up in his own bed, and he lay there in a morphine haze. I was with him that morning when he suddenly woke up and looked at me with a lucidity I hadn't seen in weeks. It was as if he interrupted his free fall and paused, suspended in the air for just a moment. We stared at each other for a few minutes. I had never seen him so afraid. Then his eyes closed, forever.

I saw that same look on Mike's face.

The coroner's building was a burgundy brick structure with front steps flanked by the kind of large, globe-topped lamps that made it feel like the local library. I half expected a cheery volunteer to tell me where the card catalogue was located when I entered. Instead, Detective Ricohr led me down a long corridor to a viewing room not far from the refrigerators that held the bodies. The procedure was a blur, save for the one recollection that I wished I didn't remember.

Hours later, still nursing a drink at the bar in Union Station, I couldn't get that image out of my head. I drifted back to the time of my father's death. The day after he passed, I asked Claire to marry me. Sitting there in the train station, I had that same fear as when I had made that decision—a fear of never wanting to be alone.

"…I'm sorry," Cheli whispered as we hugged.

The waiter came over, but she waved him off.

"So what do they have?" I asked.

Cheli studied me and realized I was desperate for the details.

"He was shot with a nine millimeter. We know that much from the casing found underneath the car. All the calls on his cell leading up to the murder were to you or to his office. The detectives are following up on some other ideas, but there isn't a lot of hope it will bring much."

"What do you think of this Detective Lopez?"

"He doesn't think much of you. But he's a good detective."

I would have felt better with Ricohr.

"Mike's cell phone was still in the car? What about his wallet?"

Cheli nodded.

"Then it wasn't a robbery."

"We don't know that for sure," she corrected.

"It has to be connected to the Arroyo."

"Chuck, we can't know that."

"What else could it be? They should be checking every building in that area for some connection back to Valenti and his crew. Probably building another concept mall or some equally useless development." I was angry at that old man and his manipulation of the strings that ran Los Angeles. "Are you at least going to talk to them?"

Her silence was my answer.

"It's not pointing that way," she said cryptically.

"Which way is it pointing?"

"Mike ever use drugs?"

"Just Bushmills. Why?"

"In a search of the car, the police found a small bag of OxyContin, about ten pills. They already checked his records, and Mike didn't have a prescription for them."

"Mike wasn't popping pills."

"He was murdered a block off the 10 Freeway. It's common in that area to have the buy take place close to the off-ramp. His window was down so he was speaking to someone—"

"Let me guess. Detective Lopez's theory?"

"'I'm just stating the facts," she said. "I'm not making any conclusions."

"So you believe it, too."

"He has been after this story for weeks," she started. "You said it yourself that he drives himself into the ground when he gets a good story. Maybe he wants to come back down after charging hard for so long. Maybe he's been addicted all this time but he hid it from you. How well do you really know him, Chuck? We all think we know each other, but in reality we know so little."

She was starting to convince me, and I hated myself for it.

"But my opinion doesn't matter," she continued, "I'm not on the case, remember? This is LA Homicide, not Glendale. I'm just a bystander, like you."

I couldn't tell if Cheli's frustration was born out of an inability to help me or because she was sidelined in a case that mattered. Perhaps it was a little bit of both.

The rush of travelers slowed as the dying summer sun dimmed in the windows. The wall sconces clicked on and cast the station in a sort of weary sadness.

"All these people rushing off…" Cheli observed, leaving out whatever unsatisfactory conclusion should finish it. "I'll take that drink now," she said.

When we both had fresh drinks, we raised our glasses in a toast to Mike. The alcohol helped bring some reason back into my head.

"I guess I have to acknowledge one flaw in my theory," I said.

"What's that?"

"If this is one big, long chain like I believe, with Valenti sitting at the top as the puppet master, he couldn't have had Mike killed."

"Why not?"

"Because his hired gun is sitting in a Glendale jail."

Cheli's eyes narrowed.

"He was released on Wednesday," she said.

"He was? Why?"

"Because the DA didn't think we had enough to

get a conviction," she said, and I could tell it pained her to admit it. "She said we jumped the gun on the arrest." Although Cheli used the plural article it was clear that criticism was directed solely at her. "I'll get him," she resolved.

"So Temekian had the opportunity to kill Mike. Now what?"

"Run a ballistics test on the gun that killed Langford with the one that killed Mike. Same shooter, same gun."

WHISPERING PINES

At the very south end of Glendale, on a series of rolling hills dotted with acacias, black oaks, and towering pines, sits an expansive cemetery. A century ago, the vision of a dreamer turned these scrabbled hills into a peaceful stretch of land with more shade per square inch than anywhere in the city outside of a parking garage. Ponds are well stocked with cattails and wading birds. Statuary dots the landscape with endless portrayals of nymphs and cherubs and other half-naked figures. It's a fabricated landscape that feels as authentic as anything Walt Disney could have dreamed up.

I grew up dreading cemeteries, with their tall granite walls dripping green-gray with moss and their headstones fighting hopelessly against the pull of gravity. But here you were instructed to find inspiration. Each knoll was themed and clearly marked with signage to clue visitors, and permanent residents, where they were. "Sunrise Slope" naturally faced east toward the dawn of day. "Everlasting Love" stood in the shadow of hundred-year-old oaks, while "Slumberland" was a quiet recess nestled on the northern slope, where you had to strain your ears to hear even the faintest trace of traffic noise. "Babyland" was a stretch no one should ever have to visit in his lifetime.

Mike's final resting place was in a section called "Wee Kirk o' the Heather," a name shared with one of the early and famous wedding chapels in Las Vegas. Mike would have found that amusing. An aunt on his mother's side picked it out and made all the arrangements. Mike didn't have any close family, and I was grateful that this sweet woman did all of the planning. There was a short service in a small stone church that was said to be patterned off some famous village landmark in Scotland. It held ninety, but only fifteen showed up. You could easily spot his journalist friends with their extended waistlines, sallow skin, and suits that looked like they'd been rolled in balls and stored in steamer trunks. There was little fanfare around Mike's murder, despite his being somewhat of a public figure. He was a legitimate journalist for a small-time rag. Perhaps if he'd been a fixture on the local channels he'd have elicited a larger showing.

After the service, Cheli and I and the small group of mourners moved outside, where a perfectly dug hole awaited. I marveled at how precise the sides of the hollowed-out earth were and wondered what kind of machine was used to create that. A few more words were spoken, and then the casket was lowered slowly into the ground. More words, a few spoonfuls of dirt from a pristine hand trowel, and the whole thing was over.

Mike's elderly aunt thanked me for coming and apologized for having to rush off. She lived in Lancaster and wanted to get on the road before traffic hit. Soon enough it was just me, Cheli, and the groundskeepers. Out of respect, they had patiently waited for the entire party to disperse before concluding the job. We headed back to our cars to give them the space they needed to finish burying my friend. Leaning against the hood of my car was Detective Ricohr.

"You were right," he said to Cheli. "The bullets match."

I studied his face. "What else?"

"The lab came back with some partial prints on the bag that held the pills. They won't hold up in court, but it's enough to ID the person."

"Temekian?" she asked.

"We have a warrant out, but he's disappeared. He won't get far."

"No he won't," she confirmed. "Sounds like we're teaming up on this?"

"We both want the same guy," Ricohr acknowledged.

"Then let's get after it," she said.

I called out to them as they walked off. "Put the screws to him. I bet he gives up Valenti."

"There's no proof of any link between them," he reminded me.

"He'll talk. Trust me."

As I was about to get into my car, I saw Claire across the way. She must have been standing there for a while. She walked over and joined me.

"Did you stay for the service?" I asked.

"I watched it from the road," she said, tugging at her shirtsleeve. "I wanted to call you but, I don't know…I wasn't sure you wanted to hear from me. When we last talked, I said some things that I regret. I know you were his friend. I'm sorry, Chuck."

"I'm glad you came," I told her. That seemed to put her a little at ease. She leaned against the car by me.

"What is all this mess? All these people dying?"

"I don't know. The police are still trying to figure it out."

"Do you think Valenti is involved?"

"Yes, but no one really knows."

"I can't fathom how he could be," she said, but her tone said she was starting to believe it. "You need to walk away and let the police handle it. Or you're just going to get yourself killed."

The last part sounded like a wife's voice, something I hadn't heard in a long time and now realized how much I missed.

We stayed there for a few moments, taking in the expanse of manicured lawns that seem to roll effortlessly off each hill. Down a short distance was a row of majestic pine trees that swayed gently in the afternoon breeze.

"What a strange place," she said.

Temekian seemed to have melted away in the summer sun. Rumors abounded that he slipped out of the country through Mexico and was back in Armenia or Russia, but none of the rumors could be substantiated. Cheli gave me updates when she had them, but after the first few days they grew less frequent to the point that two weeks later when we met, we barely talked about it.

"They're freezing me out," she told me after the second glass of wine. I knew she was in a sour mood the moment she arrived at my apartment. It took my asking her for a progress report on Temekian to bring it all out.

"Who is?" I asked.

"Everyone. Ricohr, that fat tub Lopez, the Feds. They're all fucking me over." I stayed silent to allow time for her to cool down. Instead, she looked at me contemptuously. "You don't like this side of me, do you?"

"I didn't say anything."

"You didn't have to. I don't like it either, but you do what you have to in order to succeed," she said in an attempt to explain herself.

"I'm having trouble following you."

"They took me off the case," she blurted out, "and assigned some idiot to take my place."

"Which case?"

"Temekian's prescription drug ring. They say the Feds wanted to take the lead because of the Medicare fraud angle, but I know they wanted results and apparently I wasn't able to deliver them. I think that DA had it in for me. There was room for only one chick on that job and she didn't want me taking all the camera time. Not that she was camera-ready," she added nastily. "I guess I deserved it for jumping the gun with the Temekian arrest. Someone in my situation can't be making mistakes like these for long."

"You're being too hard on yourself."

"Am I?" she shot back.

"Yeah, and it's crossing over into self-pity. That's the side of you I don't like."

At least I managed to eke a smile out of her.

"I want to get drunk, Chuck. Will you get drunk with me?"

"Sure." I moved to the kitchen to open another bottle.

"Where's your neighbor with the music?" Cheli called from the living room. "I'm in the mood for the old, sad ones!"

"He usually doesn't come on stage until after ten," I shot back. I tossed the empty bottle into the recycling bin that was already overflowing with newspapers and cans. It couldn't possibly take any more, so I hefted the crate and slipped out the back door of the kitchen to where the large bins were lined up in the alley. I created such a ruckus emptying the contents that I never heard him approaching behind me.

"Hey," he said and put a heavy hand on my shoulder.

I nearly spun out of my shoes when I saw him—the unmistakable mug of the brute who'd kicked in my ribs a few weeks back. He was alone this time, except for the gun he clutched in the hand that wasn't digging into my shoulder. I was about to shout, but he raised the gun toward my lips, instantly silencing them.

"Shut up," he said. "Shut up and you don't get hurt."

I assumed that the reason I wasn't lying face down in a pool of my own blood was that he hadn't come to kill me.

"What do you want?" I asked quietly.

"They say we can trust you," he began.

"Who's *we*?"

"Ardavan didn't kill those people they say he killed."

"You've spoken to him?"

"Someone has."

"If he didn't kill anyone, tell him to turn himself in to the authorities so he can clear his name. Why the disappearing act?"

The thug shook his head like an ape. "Can't trust them."

"You can't trust whom? The police?"

"He wants to make a deal," he announced.

"You just told me he didn't kill anyone but now he wants to negotiate a plea?"

"He knows things," he droned.

"Knows things about what?" I shot back, annoyed. The fragmented speech grated on me. It showed in my voice. "Make some sense."

"He knows what happened to Vadaresian." The hairs on the back of my neck pricked up. "He was there when he got killed."

"Where?"

"At that building," he answered but exactly which building I was not sure. "Ardavan wants a deal."

"Look, I'm not a lawyer and I'm not the police. I can't be making deals. Even if I could, they wouldn't amount to anything. He needs to turn himself in, and if all that you say is true, then he can work out some kind of deal."

"He is afraid. He wants you to meet him and then he will go to the police. He will call you with the time and place."

"Chuck?" Cheli's voice rang out from the back door of the apartment. "Where are you?"

The thug was already backing up.

"Where was Vadaresian killed?" I whispered after him.

"I told you," he replied. "At that building."

The thug took off running toward the end of the alley. He curved around the corner and disappeared into the night.

"What's going on?" Cheli asked me.

"I think I know where Ed is," I answered.

CADILLAC MAN

Having been stripped of her role on the prescription drug case, Cheli threw everything she had at the one case left that mattered—Ed's disappearance.

Five minutes after my encounter in the alley, Cheli was already working the phone. The first call was to another detective in her department. The second was to Detective Ricohr to discuss how we wanted to approach the Temekian meeting. She then called a sit-down for the next day with the head of Glendale homicide. She was going to make a big request of him. "He's not going to like it, but he better damn well give it to me," she told me as she hurried out of the apartment.

Her request was expensive, and it wasn't immediately approved the next day. Cheli wanted a cadaver dog and excavation equipment to find Ed's body at the Deakins Building and dig it up. Both came with big price tags. Her director initially balked at the idea due to a combination of a tight budget and Cheli's recent failures. There was also the issue of the building explicitly being named by Temekian's associate.

"He said 'that' building, right?" Cheli grilled me for the hundredth time after the alley encounter. "He didn't say 'the' building but 'that' building."

"Correct, he said 'that.' "

"It has to be Deakins," she stated.

"Are you sure?"

That's exactly the question she got from everyone she spoke to. And the more she answered it, the more convinced she became. One day turned into two and still no approval. At one point Cheli offered to pay for some of the services out of her own pocket. There still was no approval. Another day passed, and then I got the call.

"Tomorrow, 8 a.m."

"You got the approval?"

"I can't talk now," she whispered. "Let's just say I played the Latina card and it worked." The power of a racial discrimination lawsuit again proved its worth. At least this time it was for a good cause. "See you in the morning."

The following day we gathered at the Deakins Building. It was a cool, gray morning with a thick layer of cloud cover that seemed to press down on the entire city. I sipped coffee from outside the fence and watched the proceedings.

There were several pickup trucks with industrial toolboxes in their beds. An excavator like the kind you rent at a home center idled out in the street. The diggers wore fluorescent vests and hard hats. The detectives wore suits and tried not to muddy their shoes. It had all started here and hopefully it was going to end here.

Ed's father-in-law arrived a short while after I did. He was accompanied by another Armenian man, who looked like his brother. Rafi was not with them. I had left several unanswered messages on his phone. I'd even driven out to Glendale to the place he'd been staying, but he wasn't home. The message I'd left with the woman who answered the door got no response.

I caught eyes with the old man, and he came over to greet me. We shook hands. He looked to the sky at the gray blanket and said, "I hope it is over after today."

I nodded and placed a supportive hand on his shoulder. His brother silently led him back to the car.

The man of the hour, or rather the beast of the hour, was a sweet-looking yellow lab from a volunteer sheriff's group called LA Search Dogs. They assisted with earthquake rescues and the occasional lost hiker who got turned around in the miles of trails in the mountains of Los Angeles. They also helped with cadaver searches.

"She loves things that smell bad," I overheard her handler say to one of the uniformed police officers. The lab was outfitted in a canvas vest and short leash. She was anxious to explore the grounds but had to cool her heels while the crime scene unit methodically went through their instructions on how the process was going to work. In short, stay off the grounds and let them handle it.

Cheli was in the lead, but I could tell she was anxious. She crossed her arms tightly over her chest, and when I asked about it, she made a comment about the cool weather. It was left unsaid between us, but we knew that a mistake here was going to cost her her career.

"All right," she announced to the group once the CSI unit was done with its introduction, "let's bring the dog in."

The group created an opening for the yellow lab and her handler to pass. There was an initial excitement as the dog began sniffing around the fence and the area directly beyond the main gate. The handler had divided the area into a grid with zones and sub-zones and methodically worked the dog over each. It was agonizing to watch. With each jerk of the dog's head the group collectively leaned forward to see if this was finally it. Every time, though, it was a dead bird or a half-eaten chicken wing, in which case the handler had to scold her dog before continuing with the search. The novelty wore off quickly, and the gawkers at the fence turned their attention to their phones, and some drifted back to their trucks for a quick nap.

Cheli surveyed the scene with some other detectives from the force. No one did much talking, least of all Cheli, who stood stoically. It pained me to watch her watch the search. It was as if she was willing with all her strength for that dog to find something to prove her right. The longer the search went without results, the smaller the group around her became. The detectives melted away and formed other groups, smaller this time. Their collective gaze gradually shifted from the yellow lab and her handler to Cheli, who in a mere forty-five minutes went from the center of attention to a solitary figure standing off to the side.

There was something in the man's gait that caught my attention. The cadaver crew had changed dogs and had moved to the back of the building out of our sightline from the street. Most of the bystanders were elsewhere, and I was left alone at the fence. I saw the man come around the corner and quickstep it over to an unmarked police car, where he furiously began typing into the unit's computer. I shifted my gaze back to the building, from which more people emerged. They were animated and started barking out orders to some of the excavation crew. The old man suddenly appeared at my side and strained his eyes to see what was going on across the way.

"Is this it?" he asked me.

At that moment Cheli appeared from behind the building. Her arms were no longer crossed tightly across her chest. He hands now sat squarely on her hips as she spoke to another detective. We caught eyes, and she gave me a brief nod and an even briefer smile.

"I think it is," I told the old man.

They played that same overhead shot on loop for the better part of the day. It showed nothing other than a few dark figures scurrying in and out of a giant, white tent that covered the spot where they found the body. I watched the rest of the proceedings on the TV in my apartment. The news had no information but still dedicated the majority of the broadcast to the story. As I watched the image of a black plastic body bag being wheeled out to a coroner's van, I hoped this wasn't how Rafi would find out about his father.

Everything fell into place quickly from there. The family produced dental records, which they matched to the body found at the Deakins Building and thus confirmed the identification. The coroner concluded that

Ed had died from a single shot to the back of the head. He also suffered blunt force trauma to the base of the skull before he was shot. Ballistics was able to recover the bullet that killed him, and it matched the gun that was used to kill both Langford and Mike. Ed had been buried in a shallow grave in a recess behind the building. No other evidence of any significance was recovered from the scene. Ed's case was officially changed to a homicide.

The attention then shifted to me. Three days had passed and still there was no attempt to contact me by any of Temekian's people. I was given twenty-four-hour surveillance and a dedicated patrolman who watched over my block.

Not wanting the unnecessary attention of constant police presence in and around my office, the senior executives decided it was prudent to grant me an extended leave from work. They were very accommodating, particularly when I pitched it as unpaid leave. I knew enough not to force their hand, and saving the firm money was always the easiest path to ingratiating myself with senior execs.

I had endless conversations with detectives from both the Glendale and Los Angeles forces and even longer discussions with a police psychologist, who briefed me on the nuances of negotiations. I wanted to tell him this wasn't anything I didn't already know from my years in human resources, but he seemed so proud of his skill set that I let him think he, and he alone, owned it.

I didn't see much of Cheli during that time, outside of the official meetings we had regarding the case. She went from persona non grata to lead investigator in a matter of hours. It was a stunning reversal, and the capper would be to bring Temekian in for the three murders. I was both elated at her turnaround and disappointed that it came at the expense of our time together.

The authorities eventually released Ed's body to his family. A full service was held two days later, and I reluctantly found myself back at the same cemetery where Mike was buried.

Ed's service was a much grander affair. A long procession of cars made its way through the imposing iron gates on a late Wednesday morning. The car that held the coffin slowly wound its way up the main lane and dipped and rose from knoll to knoll until coming to rest at the back side of the cemetery on "Resurrection Slope," which overlooked Highland Park.

Swarms of dark suits and black dresses tromped down the blue-green hill to the gravesite and left dark footprints in the wet grass. Ed's father-in-law got lost in a whirlwind of hugs and double-kisses. He was clearly the chief mourner of the day. It took me some searching from the roadside to spot Rafi. The boy stood apart from the main group and watched the proceedings like an outsider, even though it was his father they were putting to rest. I made my way down the hill and sidled up to him.

"I'm sorry for your loss," I told him and extended a hand, which he took casually in his. He kept his eyes fixed on the group surrounding his grandfather.

"Papik is in all his glory today," he said. "He spared no expense on the service. Look at the flowers, the casket. I think he even paid for the silk lining, even though no one would see it. Were you at the memorial dinner?" he asked me, knowing that I wasn't. "You should have been. What a spread. We closed down Carousel Restaurant on a Saturday night. Everyone gave speeches. It was touching."

"They're going to get the people who did this to your father," I said.

Rafi finally pulled his gaze from the mourners to look at me. "What does it matter when they do?" he asked. "Does it change anything?"

"Probably not, but it can give you some closure."

"I never heard that word until my father went missing. I'm not sure what it means."

I regretted the use of the mourning clichés. Rafi didn't hold it against me, but I had hoped I could have been more supportive and not just another babbling, amateur psychotherapist talking about grief and overcoming loss. The boy was in a precarious spot. Parentless at a young age, growing further away from the extended family, and already showing signs of being resigned to what life had dealt him.

"Was that lawyer able to help you?"

"In the end I decided not to call him," he told me. "It's just money. I'll be all right without it."

It was the first thing he said that wasn't tinged with anger or resentment. It was the kind of decision that tends to come at an age much older than Rafi's—some people just have to grow up faster than others. Rafi said he would be fine, and I believed him. I offered my help and told him to call me whenever he wanted. He thanked me. As I walked off to join the others, he called back to me.

"You know he wasn't perfect," he said.

"Nobody's perfect," I told him.

"But he was a good guy?" he said more as a question than a statement, like he was searching for validation to a belief long held but never uttered.

"Your father was a good man."

Rafi took it in, then joined the others. I watched him move next to an older woman in a dark dress and coat. They spoke a little, and then he let himself get wrapped tightly in her arms.

After the service, I crossed over the hill to where Mike was buried. The sun had burned off the marine layer, and it dappled the lawns with patches of gold. This was the most death I had been around in my life. And I didn't like it. Anything in excess, even exhilaration, will eventually make you sick. I turned around before I got to Mike's grave. I wanted to be around the living again.

As I returned to my car, I noticed a solitary figure standing under one of the giant pine trees. It was Ed's father-in-law. All of the mourners had dispersed, but he remained behind. He used the tree's trunk to help steady himself as he looked out over the city. From that spot he was able to look across at all of the major hills on the eastern side of Los Angeles: Montecito Heights at the bottom, then moving north to Mount Washington, Highland Park and Altadena, La Cañada high up in the foothills, and finally, the Glendale highlands. The thousands of houses that dotted the hillsides sparkled in the fresh morning light. The old man gazed at them for a long time. He then shook whatever thoughts had entered his mind and slowly made his way back down to his car.

It was a valiant effort, but he couldn't mask his disappointment; he still looked like someone who had to return a Cadillac.

THAT COLOGNE AGAIN

I got the text later that day.

"It doesn't smell right," Detective Lopez commented as we huddled in my living room. This was the first time I'd had more guests than there were chairs for everyone to sit. Cheli paced the room like an anxious cat, while Detective Ricohr spoke with someone on the phone in the kitchen.

The text simply stated an address and time. The address was a home-improvement store in Burbank, and the time was to be several hours after they closed.

"An empty parking lot makes total sense—" Cheli started to explain, but Detective Lopez didn't let her finish.

"Anything?" he asked Ricohr, who'd returned from the kitchen.

"Not a registered number," he replied. "Looks like a pay-as-you-go phone."

"He wants to see if Mr. Restic is alone," Cheli continued.

"The man is turning himself in," Detective Lopez countered. "Why would he care if this fellow here is alone or has the entire LAPD behind him? We're supposed to be worried about his motives, but he seems more worried about ours."

"He thinks he's being scapegoated," I added.

"A scapegoat doesn't have all the evidence pointing his way," Cheli replied. "He's the lead suspect and a goddamn good one."

"Which is why I don't like this," Lopez said. "When something doesn't add up there's usually a reason. Why you?" he shot in my direction.

"He knows him," Cheli answered for me.

"Let him speak for himself, detective. Why did he contact you, Mr. Restic?"

"I've met Temekian a few times. He knows I was working with Ed's family. He also knows I've uncovered information about him."

"He also sent his boys to straighten out your teeth," Lopez added. "And now you're such close friends that he trusts you to orchestrate his surrender?"

It was hard to overlook the skepticism in his voice.

"Why does every question you ask me sound like an accusation?"

"I'm sorry if you're interpreting it that way."

"Come off it, Detective," Cheli shot back. "You know what you're doing and it stinks."

"Enlighten me."

"You have some hunch Mr. Restic is involved in these murders but you don't know how, and instead of doing the hard work it takes to figure it out, you sit back and throw barbs and hope he says something wrong. That's not good police work."

"What do you think, Terry?" Lopez asked Ricohr.

"Who cares what he thinks!" Cheli exploded. "You can't just sit here and blow me off like this. We're on a joint task force between our departments. Let me know if you don't know what the word 'cooperation' means and I will help enlighten you."

"Detective, I am just asking for someone's opinion. Let's not start a war over nothing." Lopez turned back to Ricohr. "Well?"

"I'm not sure."

"There's some deep thinking," she muttered under her breath, which hopefully only I could hear. Ricohr didn't take any offense.

"I say we go there with numbers and take him down and see what he has to say in the room, like Detective Alvarado has suggested."

"Finally," Cheli breathed dramatically.

"Okay," Lopez said, slapping his knee and rising to his feet. "Let's talk about how we want to bring him in."

Cooler heads gathered around the coffee table and drew up the plan. I was to meet Temekian at the requested time in the parking lot. We worked out a signal for the detectives and uniformed officers who would be close by should I need assistance. I was instructed not to get into any car and not to let Temekian into mine. We were to leave in separate vehicles and drive to the station on Western Avenue. We, naturally, would never make it that far. Units would move in to take Temekian into custody as soon as he exited the parking lot.

The detectives were meticulous in the details—they prepared a brief for the other officers that had all the information they could possibly need, including whether I was to be clean-shaven or with the slight stubble I was currently sporting. I made a note to shave before leaving for the rendezvous. I took comfort in the details, as if a long list of minutiae applied some sort of order to the chaos around me. If the three detectives had simply slapped their hands and said, "Let's do this" without poring over a drawn-out plan, I would have felt a lot worse.

We adjourned with a plan to meet at the high school parking lot a half-hour before the scheduled meeting time. We'd then go over last-minute instructions before proceeding to the home-improvement store. As everyone filed out, Cheli affectionately tousled my hair and gave some quiet words of encouragement, but they weren't quiet enough—I noticed Detective Ricohr catch the gesture out of the corner of his eye. He didn't say anything.

I took a long, hot shower and shaved. After twenty years of shaving every morning at roughly the same time, an evening version of the same activity felt foreign. Even my face rejected the change in routine in the form of several rosebuds on my neck. I dressed in a shirt Claire had bought me for Christmas—the loudest, brightest shirt I owned and one I never wore. I headed out early in case there was traffic. There was always traffic.

It was the unmistakable combination of burnt orange and diesel that initially gave me pause. I was instantly brought back to that afternoon in my office—Ed admitting he used the Resting Room for personal calls, wiping away a tear with his thick, hairy finger, calling me "Mr. Restic." For a few seconds I was actually there in my office. But what I struggled to comprehend was why the smell of Ed's awful cologne was now in my own car.

Then came the voice from behind me.

I was so startled my foot jammed down the accelerator and the engine whined in a piercing shriek as only a hybrid car can do. Luckily, I was still in park or I'd have driven the car right through my neighbor's fence and into his chicken coop.

"Take it easy," Temekian instructed. "Just do what you were supposed to do."

"I'm not sure what that is," I said.

"What did the cops tell you?"

"We're meeting at the Burbank High School parking lot."

"What time?"

"Nine-thirty."

"We have time. Take the 5," he instructed. "And give me your cell phone."

I fished my phone out of my pocket and handed it to him. He was scrunched down on the floor of the car with his feet extended to the spot directly behind me. In that position he had a clear angle of me and could watch all of my moves.

We took Griffin over to the freeway on-ramp. There was a bottleneck at this portion of the freeway where the road dipped and curved around downtown and crossed two major mergers with the Santa Monica Freeway and the Arroyo Seco Parkway. I eased my way into the sea of red taillights and inched along with the rest of the tide. The hybrid was on electric power now and unsettlingly quiet. For once I wished I had a gas-guzzler with a big engine to provide a little noise. Instead, I was left to contemplate the situation while listening to the uneven breathing coming from the back seat.

"What's going to happen tonight?" the voice asked eventually. "At the parking lot."

"I'm supposed to meet you and convince you to come with me to the Burbank police station."

"And what if I don't want to?"

I thought over my response and decided there was no use trying to make something up. "The police are going to arrest you before you get out of the lot."

"They're going to kill me," he said.

I caught a brief glimpse of Temekian, his face illuminated by a big rig's lights as it changed into our lane behind us. The rig made one more move to exit, and Temekian was again in darkness. The face I saw looked much younger than I remembered. It stared disconsolately at the car floor.

"Don't do anything foolish and you won't get hurt," I advised. "They just want to talk to you. And by foolish I mean trying to run, or fighting your way out. The word is you are armed and dangerous."

"That's what they said?" he scoffed. "Now I know they are going to kill me."

"No one is getting killed if we just do what we're supposed to do. Are you armed?" I asked.

"You think I'm going to give them an excuse to shoot me?" he answered. I assumed that meant he wasn't, but I couldn't assume he was telling the truth. It did put me a little more at ease, however.

"Why don't we just call the police and tell them I'm bringing you in."

"No. Drive to Burbank like I said."

We crawled along a little farther then came to a dead stop.

"Why do you think they're going to kill you?" I asked.

"Because they are in on it."

"In on what?"

"Everything," he said.

My mind raced with possibilities. It was well established that Valenti's influence extended deep into the power structure of this city, but it had never crossed my mind that it might include the police. It was a fantastic allegation but one I couldn't dismiss outright. I rattled off the names of the players, from Valenti to Claire to McIntyre—anyone who was remotely connected to Ed's disappearance. Nothing registered until I got to one name.

"Yeah, I worked with him," Temekian responded when I asked him about Langford. "I helped him on some jobs. He fixed up apartments in bad neighborhoods and sometimes there were people living there who didn't want to get out."

"So you helped them. Is this what you did on Holcomb?"

"Yeah, that fat guy was stubborn." He laughed. "Took four of us to get him off that chair. He sweated so much he was slippery to hold onto. Big fat fish on the floor."

"Why did Langford buy those buildings?"

"I don't know. Because he wanted to make money?"

"Was he buying for someone else? Does the name Salas mean anything to you?"

"Salas? No, I don't know a Salas. Langford paid me in cash, and that's all I care about."

"Did Langford hire you to work on Ed?" I asked. This time Temekian was silent, so quiet that I glanced into the back seat to see if he was still there. "What happened to Ed?" I repeated.

"They want to blame me for everything," he said, sulking.

Over the years in my role in Human Resources, I'd noticed a trend among the guilty; they would succumb to a sickening level of self-pity in the moments immediately after being caught. We labeled it "WIM" for "woe is me." During WIM, associates would lament the decisions that got them there and then apply those decisions to some seemingly long list of misfortunes they had suffered. While admitting fault, they also deflected blame by attaching their actions to some higher force at play. Listening to Temekian sulk felt like textbook WIM.

"Did you kill Ed?" I asked. After a prolonged silence, I said, "Answer the question."

"I was there," he said noncommittally.

"Where? The Deakins Building?"

"Yeah. I asked him to meet me there."

"Why?"

"Because he was being a pain in the ass about the deal. I was just going to scare him a bit. Tell him it was better to sell."

"Did Langford ask you to bring him there?" I asked.

"Yes."

"Was he there when Ed was killed?"

"No, he wasn't there."

"Who else was there?"

"I didn't shoot him," he said instead of answering. "I hit him but I didn't shoot him. I never killed no one."

"Langford. Did you kill Langford?"

"No, no—"

"What about Mike Wagner?" Again he denied it.

"If you didn't kill these people, then someone else did. Who was it?"

"They're going to kill me," he repeated.

"Who is? Who is going to kill you?"

Temekian was becoming more and more distraught. He looked like a man who hadn't slept in days. I kept the pressure on and repeatedly asked him more and more questions, but he slipped into a mumbling mess, all crumpled up on the backseat floor. At one point, he erratically reached for the door handle and tried to get out of the car. The child safety locks for the children we never had kept him inside.

"Take it easy," I told him in a soothing voice. "Take it easy, okay?"

"I'm tired," he said.

"Okay, just take it easy."

As we moved past Dodger Stadium the traffic eased up and cars began jockeying for position for the frantic rush out into the Valley. I stayed in the slow lane.

"I need help," he said. "Rafi told me that you know lawyers. I need a white one, someone I can trust. I don't want no Armenian. They're crooks."

The blanket condemnation of Armenian lawyers was telling. He knew how to navigate the system enough to steal from it but when it came time to legitimately manipulate it for his right to a defense, he was completely lost.

I was torn between two duties—the one I had with the authorities to fulfill our commitment of delivering a suspected criminal, and the one I had to a man who, according to the rule of law, was still innocent and had the right and need to prove it.

"I can make some calls," I told him.

We pulled off the freeway at Colorado and swung around into Glendale. There was a run-down motor lodge not far from the exit. It was a remnant of the pre-freeway days when Colorado was still a major throughway. I pulled into the parking lot it shared with a small doughnut shop.

"Let's get a coffee and talk options," I said.

I stepped out into the sparsely populated lot. As I shut my door I heard a voice call out from behind me.

"What are you doing?" Cheli asked as she got out of her car.

Just then Temekian stumbled out of the back seat. He looked up and saw Cheli. His eyes flashed as he shouted out something in Russian.

"Don't move!" Cheli shouted as she positioned herself behind her car door. She pulled her gun and trained it on Temekian.

Temekian shot me a look filled with contempt as if I had lured him into this trap he was now in. Although I'd done nothing, I felt like I had betrayed him.

"Cheli, wait!" I implored. Turning back to Temekian I could see him contemplating his next move. "Hold on. Don't do anything—"

But he bolted toward the back of the motor lodge before I could finish. Cheli immediately gave chase, and I was left powerless to do anything other than watch. I drifted slowly in the direction of the pursuit. Temekian whipped around the back corner and disappeared into the darkened alley behind the lodge. Cheli threw herself into the corner of the building, carefully peeked around, and then took off after him.

The night receptionist cautiously poked his head out from the lobby.

"Call 911!" I told him. "Tell them there's a—"

A shot rang out. The hotel clerk and I shared a look but neither of us made a move. A few seconds later there was another shot. This time the clerk ran back inside to call the police.

A FINE MESS

I crept along the walkway between the lower floor of motel rooms and the parking spots immediately in front of them. The few people who were staying there peered out through dusty blinds, but no one dared venture out from behind their doors. Apparently they knew a gunshot when they heard one. When I got to the back corner I did like Cheli and slowly peered into the dark alley. I let my eyes adjust to the change in light but still could not discern any movement.

Using the building as my guide, I worked my way deeper into the alley where dumpsters and a cinderblock wall framed out the one-lane stretch. At the far end busy Pacific Avenue glowed with the passing headlights. Suddenly, a figure in silhouette appeared from behind one of the dumpsters. It held a gun and scanned the alley. Then it saw me and turned and walked in my direction.

My head said stay and confront the figure, but my feet said run like hell. I tripped over part of an old engine block. Scrambling to my feet—

"Chuck!"

Cheli hurried over to me.

"He's dead. I need to call this in," she said, and dashed off to her car.

My eyes went back toward the dumpster where I could now see two feet protruding from behind it. Curiosity drove me closer. I kept my distance but angled around the dumpster to get a look at him. He looked deflated. His head and arms were in an unnatural position that you see only with the deceased. His eyes were open. I then noticed the shiny black pool that began from under his torso and formed a rivulet that bent and banked all the way toward me.

"What are you doing?" Cheli shrieked, returning to the alley. "You're standing in the blood."

I had stepped into the stream, which now coursed around me like a real river would around a boulder. Cheli pulled me away from the scene and led me back toward the parking lot.

"I'll stay with the body. You go wait out front for the arriving officers," she instructed. "Tell them I'm back here. I don't want some hothead to shoot me."

The sounds of the sirens signaled to the people behind the dusty blinds that it might be safe to come out. A pool of bystanders congregated near the front office. The first patrol car roared around the corner and nearly took out a minivan whose driver was surprised by the sudden flashing lights. The young officers jumped out of the car at the main entrance to the lobby; one unholstered his pistol, while the other held a shotgun. The clerk pointed to the back of the building and they sprinted off in that direction. I shouted that Cheli was back there, but they never heard me as two more patrol cars came bearing down on us from the opposite direction and drowned out my voice.

Luckily, I heard no more shooting, and Cheli eventually emerged from the back alley with the two officers in tow. She barked out a few orders that sent them scurrying off to do some thankless job, but happy to do it and feel like they were part of something important.

The scene devolved into a chaotic mess. The drivers of each responding patrol car insisted on keeping their lights flashing despite the lack of a need to do it. News choppers descended and hovered noisily overhead. The crowd of onlookers grew to the size of a small mob but was held back by the sanctity of the yellow tape.

"What happened?" Detective Ricohr asked and immediately noticed the blood on my shoe. "How'd you get that?"

I started to explain, but he waved me off and beckoned me to follow him back into the alley. Camera flashes lit up the scene. This was Glendale PD's territory, but Detective Ricohr barreled into it like it was his own.

"Who shot him?" he asked one of the patrol officers.

"Detective Alvarado."

"Temekian had jumped into my car—" I started to explain, but Ricohr interrupted me.

"Get a lawyer before you talk."

We walked into the alley together. Ricohr stopped and surveyed the scene. People were everywhere. Some searched the area with flashlights, but most congregated in small circles and milled around. At the far end of the alley a news van ran a live feed with a thousand-foot zoom lens. Ricohr sighed heavily enough to be heard over the thumping of the helicopter blades.

"We have ourselves a fine mess, don't we?" he said.

In a nation increasingly uncomfortable with police-involved shootings, the Southland held tightly to its record of quick-to-draw shootings and very high kill ratios. Protests were muted or nonexistent. By and large, the people of the city accepted the violence as a necessary by-product of the work required to keep them safe.

The shooting of Temekian was met with the same apathy. Only dedicated readers of the *LA Times* Crime Blog got any details of the incident. By the limited number of comments posted under the article, I inferred it was a small group.

Standard procedure dictated that Cheli be put on paid administrative leave pending an internal review. She sequestered herself in a cabin up in Big Bear for most of the investigation. I took my own form of administrative leave from the office, but my sequestration was self-imposed and didn't range far from my apartment in Lincoln Heights. I let the litany of friends' emails and voicemails remain unanswered.

The first few weeks were filled with long sessions with investigators from Glendale PD's internal affairs department. They asked the same questions again and again to the point that I no longer had to think of answers. The words jerked out of me as a leg jerks when prodded mercilessly with a reflex hammer. At first the investigators were curious about my involvement in all three murders. It wasn't common to have someone so closely linked to all three victims. Eventually they chalked it up to what it was—a bored corporate hack who got himself into water way over his head. Behind their assumption was an indictment, not officially stated in their report but implied in the conversations with me—I should have stayed in my office.

Cheli and I spoke very little. At first we were advised to avoid each other until the investigators had time to work through each of our stories. We did have to admit to an intimate relationship—another issue investigators repeatedly dug at but eventually saw as nothing more than a harmless tryst. We were cleared to communicate again, but something happened in those few weeks following the shooting that changed things.

Our relationship had followed the peaks and troughs of the investigation. It started with Ed's disappearance and was put to rest with Temekian's death. I began to wonder if the connection between us sprang more from our own personal doubts about bringing the case through to its conclusion, rather than any kind of real intimacy. When it all came to its violent conclusion in the alley behind the motel, there was no more oxygen for the fire to feed off and it eventually just petered out. Phone conversations were reduced to exchanges of pleasantries. They grew shorter and shallower with each one and eventually stopped altogether.

The final report issued a few weeks later came with no surprises. It was heavy on the formality and light on the personal. Detective Alvarado was cleared of criminal wrongdoing in the death of Ardavan Temekian. She had properly conducted herself under the rules of engagement outlined in Glendale's code. Temekian was a wanted criminal who was considered armed and dangerous at the time of the incident. Detective Alvarado's actions were justified, and she showed great courage in helping to apprehend the wanted fugitive.

The police officially named Temekian as the perpetrator of three murders—Bedros Vadaresian, William Langford, and Michael Wagner. Ballistics confirmed that the bullets that killed all three victims were shot by the same gun. That gun was recovered during an initial search of the alley where Temekian had been killed. He apparently had the murder weapon on him and dumped it during the pursuit with Cheli. Temekian was linked to Langford, but it never went further than that. Neither McIntyre nor Valenti—nor anyone associated with them—was ever interviewed or considered involved.

I met the official conclusion with indifference. Nothing added up. Vague threads leading back to Valenti and higher powers persisted. The idea that Mike would have stopped in that area of town and allowed Temekian to walk up to him was hard to swallow. Details on the identity of the owner of the Holcomb properties beyond the name Salas were still missing. Why McIntyre went to such great lengths to revise the zones remained a mystery. Temekian's prophecy that he would die at the hands of the police came true, but what he meant when he uttered it in my car was not clear. There were so many things to iron out, so much more work to do, so much light to shine on the dusky details of this investigation. And yet, I no longer cared.

I was wary of what would happen were I to continue searching for answers. I was fully resigned.

THE UPWARD TURN

The distractions of work had a healing effect. I found solace in the minutiae of my HR duties and jumped back into my old role with a laser-like focus.

Our operational group had recently run a cost analysis on the back-office units in Phoenix and decided that there were sizable savings if we outsourced the accounting duties to a third party. That third party, naturally, outsourced to another party and so on, until they reached a firm that was so low on the pole that there wasn't anyone below them to send the work to. This decision meant 150 people were going to be laid off.

I organized a seminar on "Dislocation Management," an overly sophisticated way of describing how human beings deal with change in their lives, which is itself another euphemism for losing their jobs. The sessions were led by an enthusiastic female duo that had parlayed an undergraduate psychology course and a natural gift for hucksterism into a lucrative consulting career. The formula they followed was pretty standard in their line of work—they took some widely understood formula, repackaged it with psycho-babble and pithy catchphrases to make it more accessible, positioned themselves as "experts" in their narrowly defined field, then let corporations pay thousands of dollars for them to impart their wisdom.

All they did was plagiarize the famous seven stages of grief and rewrite them for the corporate world. "Shock & Denial" became "Why Me?" and for "Pain & Guilt," they settled on the more personalized "What Did I Do Wrong?"

They liked rhetorical questions.

I sat in the back of the seminar room and resented the success of this dynamic duo. Their Dislocation Management seminar was no Stoplight System, but as far as these things went, their effort was a home run.

"I'm really excited about today's seminar," my co-manager Paul said, selecting the seat next to mine. "This right-sizing process is going to be very challenging," he stated solemnly but with a gleam in his eye.

"Terminations are always tough," I replied, purposefully using one of the words the duo had explicitly advised us to avoid.

"Oops, that was on the 'no-no' list," Paul warned.

"Yeah, it's hard to remember to use these made-up terms when we have all these standard ones that fit so well."

My administrative assistant rescued me from another laborious discussion with Paul. She looked annoyed.

"The girl won't leave," she huffed. "I told her to drop the package off at the mail room but she insisted on bringing it directly to you."

"Who won't leave?" I asked.

"Some bike messenger."

"How have you been?" Rosie asked as she tossed a package across to me. She had her feet up on the table again. Her messenger bag sat on the floor. She scanned my office and made a face like she disapproved.

"I didn't expect to see you again," I told her.

"Well, it's been quiet out of that office, but this package came through yesterday and I thought I'd see if you were still interested. Same deal as before."

I looked down at the package with the respective addresses for Claire's and McIntyre's firms. It seemed so long ago when I'd first intercepted their correspondence. Here was another, but it didn't have the same excitement attached to it as the previous one. I slid the package back to Rosie.

"No thanks," I told her. "I'm no longer interested."

"Would you be interested in a discount?"

"No." I laughed. "Not even at a discount."

"You look like you could use some weed."

"Nice try."

"Oh well," she said, getting to her feet. "Worth a shot."

She gathered her bag and headed for the door.

"You forgot your package," I called out.

"It's a copy," she said. "I got no use for it. You should try and incorporate some color in here," she commented on her way out. "It's too depressing."

The package sat, unopened, on my table for three days. But I never threw it out. It was a staring contest between curiosity and closure. The former won.

The package contained a four-hundred-page contract for the sale of the Deakins Building, along with several other official-looking documents with language that would require a commercial real estate broker to translate. I did my best to review the material, but the jargon made it nearly impossible to discern anything of value from it. I was thumbing through the pages when I saw the signature of an unlikely person.

※   ※   ※

"What's shaking?" my co-manager Paul asked. I had requested a quick catch-up in my office but didn't tell him the reason for it. He plopped himself into the chair and tugged at the scraggly ponytail he had worn for the last twenty years. "This is coming off next week," he announced. "I'm going buzz cut."

"That's a big change for you."

"This little guy reminds me to keep it real," he said, caressing his hair. Somehow the ponytail symbolized his closeness with nature and love for his fellow man. "But it's for a good cause."

"What do you mean?"

"I'm donating my hair to Locks of Love. They're this great nonprofit that gives free wigs to kids fighting…" he choked up for a second, then finished his thought with all the earnestness of a wake, "…cancer."

"That's admirable," I said, but didn't mean it.

"We do what we can," he intoned. "So, what'd you need from me?"

I had spent the earlier part of that morning poring over Paul's personal transactions file—the file containing the investments that we employees were required to submit—and discovered some surprising information. In the prior month, he was part of a consortium of buyers who had negotiated an agreement with the lien holders on the Deakins Building to purchase it for a reduced amount. He then sold the building to another set of investors at an amount slightly less than the one he paid in the original sale. It was a curious course of action, one that I debated internally on how to broach.

"Paul, I wanted to ask you a couple of questions, off the record, as they say."

"Uh-oh," he joked. "This sounds serious."

"Maybe, maybe not. Tell me about the Deakins Building."

That wiped the smirk off his face.

"Deakins?" he repeated, trying to buy some time. All the nuances he was trained to pick up on during his daily functions failed him at that moment when he was in the crosshairs.

"Yeah, that building you bought and sold within a month," I shot back aggressively.

"How did you hear about that, Chuck? You snooping around my personal files?"

It was another classic deflection technique.

"No and yes," I told him. "I heard about the sale and then confirmed it with the official records."

"I wish you would have come to me first. This is very inappropriate." He was reverting to corporate lingo instead of answering the question.

"Paul, this has nothing to do with you."

"It has everything to do with me."

"I mean, my interest has nothing to do with you personally. You know my involvement with Ed Vadaresian's family and all that ensued. A lot of it centered around the building you purchased, and I'm just looking to tie up some loose ends."

"I don't have any involvement with that," he said.

"I know," I replied, even if I wasn't so sure I believed him. "Can you tell me about this deal?"

"What do you want to know?"

"For starters, why did you buy the building and then immediately sell it for a loss?"

"You'll appreciate this," he said, implicating me in whatever deed he was about to describe. "This wonderful government and its complicated tax system!" He went on to describe a convoluted tale of a series of tax incentives and write-offs he got for investing in the Deakins. It involved distressed properties, manufacturing zones, brown-field zones, and many more kinds of zones. The sale at a loss added further to his side of the ledger as he could write that amount off. I understood that there was some benefit to the numerous programs the government was offering to revive a sluggish commercial real estate market, but I didn't understand how selling a building for a loss could actually result in Paul making money. "You're forgetting that I stripped out the occupancy rights," he said.

There was that phrase again. I remembered the assessor Arshalouys using it when he first spoke about the Deakins Building. He had said it like it was a desirable asset.

"What are those?" I asked.

"The city assigns every property a maximum occupancy. They literally give you a number. This is different from those signs you see at restaurants or in elevators.

Those are fire codes to keep people from being trampled. These occupancy figures are done by the city planner. It's one way they manage density. Naturally, you don't want people building willy-nilly on every inch of land," he explained, even though that seemed exactly what was done. "Nobody wants more gridlock," he added. Gridlock in their neighborhood was what they really meant.

Paul went on to explain how the process worked. If a developer wanted to build a condo on your block, he had to comply with the occupancy figure already assigned to the piece of property he wanted to build on. If his assigned number was smaller than the one he wanted for his new building, his permit would be denied. "But here's the beauty of this system," Paul said, leaning forward. "You can sell them."

"Sell what? The occupancies?"

"Yeah, I've done them a few times now. It's not very well known outside of the commercial real estate world. Even people who own property don't know it. I was just buying distressed properties from motivated sellers. But when I learned about these vouchers and that you could sell them, I lined up my investors and brushed up on the rules. You can sell them at any time to anyone you want—they are completely transferrable. The only stipulation is that they have to come from the same zone as where you plan to use them."

First property vouchers and then zones—the pieces were starting to fall into place. The zoning manipulation that Claire and McIntyre hashed out came back into the picture.

"That Deakins property was a freaking gold mine,"

said Paul, and we finally came to the part where he made his money. The man was literally salivating. He wiped his mouth with his sleeve and continued. "It was grandfathered in as a manufacturing complex, and so it had a very high number of vouchers. Apparently, this city still dreams of manufacturing jobs coming back. I sold them for a bundle."

I then asked the inevitable question. "To whom did you sell the vouchers?"

Paul squirmed in his chair. "Sorry, I'm really not at liberty to say. I'm under a strict confidentiality agreement."

"Come on, Paul, this is important."

"I'm sure it is, but so is my agreement. They were very serious about not publicizing it. And this is too good a lode to risk messing it up. I'm already telling you too much."

Paul looked intransigent. He was sitting on his gold mine and he wasn't about to do anything to tip off other prospectors in town. There was still the question, however, of how this miner found his mine.

"All right," I said. "Why the Deakins?"

"What do you mean?" he asked.

"The Deakins Building," I repeated. "How did you first hear about it? I'm just a little confused, because it's a random building in an area that I don't imagine you know much about. And coincidentally it was owned by one of our associates."

Implied, and not so subtly, in my question was the fact that Paul had to have been snooping in personnel files to even discover this building's existence. I then gambled that where there was smoke, there was fire. He had, after all, mentioned other buildings. "How did you find out about all the properties you've bought?"

The threat to unveiling his real estate transactions was grave. But it paled next to the threat of bringing down the core of his investment strategy—his job at our firm. Fifteen years from retirement, he was already in the descent mode of his career. The hard work had been done to get to this position. Now it was all about maintaining it until he finally touched down into a very comfortable retirement.

"We're friends, right?" he asked. I let the question go unanswered. There was a delectable pleasure in watching him squirm. "In a way, I was helping them," he reasoned. In Paul's logic, trolling the confidential files for associates' real estate investments and then targeting those who were underwater constituted help. "I'd help get them out from under the trouble they were in. That's how I found the Deakins. That Ed character was way overextended. When I first approached him he blew me off. He said he had some other deal going that was going to generate a lot more than the property was worth."

"That's how you found out about the occupancy vouchers."

"Yeah. He talked like he had something big going, and I was so new to the game that I just let it go."

"But once his body was discovered and ownership rights were transferred to the father-in-law you decided to revisit the transaction?"

Now it was his turn to remain silent.

"Who did you sell the vouchers to, Paul?"

THE BETTER GOOD

Valenti was gobbling up vouchers. He was undoubtedly building something in that area, but I was wrong that the Arroyo was to break ground in Lincoln Heights. In that regard, McIntyre had told me the truth when he said they had no intention of building there. But the manipulation of the zones gave me a clue where to look. Those two extra slivers of land now falling in Zone 8 were done for a reason—they didn't have the vouchers for where they wanted to build, so they adjusted the zones to include an area that was rich with them.

The picture started to come together. And the key was to follow the voucher trail. I knew the Deakins had been a target for a while, and they eventually got what they needed. As Paul so deliciously described, he'd made some "good coin" on the sale. The other slice in that pie was Carmen Hernandez's women's center. That structure also landed in the thin slivers of zone changes. Carmen had played the city and Councilman Abramian like a fiddle. She got them to buy the land for her and gave her development money to renovate the properties. But what if there was more to the deal that I was missing?

I was surprised that Carmen agreed to meet me. She'd probably linked me to the story that Mike was working on and that might eventually be published posthumously. Her off-the-record comments to Mike's request for a quote weren't fit to print even if she had given her approval. Proponents of peace and harmony often had the worst tempers. Perhaps Mike's murder had elicited some feelings of guilt and thus her acceptance of my invitation.

"Nice to see you again," Carmen greeted me warmly at the door to her office in Echo Park. She wore an embroidered floral dress with a dizzying palette of colors, the kind normally reserved for cultural parades but one that she had adopted as her everyday uniform. Carmen had sweeping arched eyebrows—they may have been drawn that way—which gave her the look of being perpetually interested in whoever was talking.

She worked in an open-plan office with several desks, copy machines, and filing cabinets. Three or four Hispanic kids, probably Chicano Studies majors, buzzed around the room with the important air of people who were "making a difference." Carmen glided through her small army of interns to an imposing desk in the back, where alley light poured in through large picture windows.

"Can someone get Mr. Restic a coffee?" she called out, even though she was a mere five feet from the coffee machine.

"I'm fine, thank you," I said and sat down in the chair

opposite the desk. Carmen took her seat and lamented at the volume of work that had to be done. She wore a wearied look. "It's for a good cause," I felt the need to add. That brought her out of her artificial sullenness.

"First things, first," she started. "Your friend. I'm sorry for your loss. We may have had our differences, but I cannot condone violence. A life is so precious, and yet the youth of today wantonly disregard it. In their defense, they know no other life than that of the streets. That's the disservice we're doing to our children in this city. There are no jobs. The schools are underfunded and underserved and out of step with the special needs of our diverse cultural potpourri." Somehow Mike's murder was a referendum on the plight of inner-city youth. "We thank the Lord they found his killer. He was an Armenian gentleman?" The racial distinction was telling. She said it like she and all other Latinos had been absolved from past sins.

"The police believe it was him, yes," I replied, but my tone said I didn't agree with it.

"The right man?" she asked.

"Maybe."

Carmen studied me. I could see her body get a little tense.

"And so what is it you wanted to discuss, Mr. Restic?" She shifted to a more formal tone.

"Relax," I tried to allay her suspicions. "I just want some information. I'm not a reporter. I have no interest in publicizing anything we discuss. I want information that could help me understand who could've had reason to kill my friend."

"I had nothing to do with it. Surely you can't think

that I did?"

"I come with no preconceived notions," I answered vaguely.

"I want to help." I waited for the *but*. "But I don't feel I should discuss this topic with you and certainly not without my legal counsel present."

"I thought you said you had nothing to do with this?"

"Who are you to accuse me?" she attacked.

"Lady, don't play this game with me. If you start throwing your weight around like you do with these stupid kids then there will be trouble."

"There's nothing to throw."

"How much did you make selling occupancy vouchers to Valenti for the properties where the new women's center is to be built?" Her cheeks turned crimson under the crimson blush. "I'll take your silence to mean that it was a fair amount."

"Can we discuss this outside?" she asked. Gone was the booming voice with the cadence of a pep rally. I leaned in and matched her tone.

"Is this volume better?" I asked. "Are you afraid your crusaders will hear that there's a cause higher than the one you've sold them? Like you said, the poor youth of today. They've yet to learn the lure and destructive nature of money."

"What do you want?" she asked coldly.

"How did the deal work? Start from the beginning. Who approached whom?"

Carmen explained the origins of the deal. It was cooked up by Langford. Like Valenti told me, everyone in a deal needs to come out in the black for it to work. Langford wanted the vouchers for the Arroyo deal. He also wanted to work a few angles on the soon-to-be women's center properties to maximize his return. He approached Carmen with the idea to have the city pay for it. He instructed her to use her connections with Councilman Abramian to ram the agreement through.

"Did the councilman know about the voucher part of the deal?" I asked.

"Did he know about that little aspect of the transaction? No. Did he and the city get a much-needed boost in a depressed area that will continue to give back to the community for decades to come? Yes," she said in a resounding fashion.

I listened to the rest of Carmen's story through the filter of knowing that the person telling the tale always told it in a favorable light as it pertained to her. Where Langford was the bully and idea man, Carmen was the babe in the woods. I imagined the truth was somewhere in the middle. And when she told me the terms of the deal, I knew it was understated. Going by the rule of thirds—whatever a gambler says he lost in Vegas is actually three times that number—the money she made on the voucher deal was a hefty sum.

"Did you know Ardavan Temekian?"

"No."

There was little emotion in her answer. It was direct and decisive. I believed her.

I was back to where I started. There was a connection between these vouchers and the murders, but the details behind it were hazy at best. Temekian seemed to fit into the play, but again I didn't know how.

I thanked Carmen for her time and honesty. She looked relieved to have it over and wanted to make sure of it by walking me to the door.

"I learned at a young age that life isn't fair," she told me. "There comes a time in all of our lives when we have to do things that may compromise what we believe is right and moral, but the larger need outweighs it. One step back, two steps forward, as they say. It's not that we are proud of it. Lord knows we aren't. But the Lord also knows the reasons why we did it and he's been known to make some exceptions." She smiled. "The larger good sometimes requires a little dirtiness so you can wash more hands. You can understand where I'm coming from."

"If that makes you feel better," I told her, "then I'm willing to go along with it."

THAT OLD ROUTINE

Claire and I met at a bar on Grand Avenue that catered to the corporate world from 5 to 9 p.m. and to the USC crowd after that. There was always a window in between when the drunken remnants of the corporate crowd intermingled with the college kids getting an early start on their partying. It was bad enough that you stayed for that fourth beer, but then to be confronted with fresh-faced youth starting out their evenings while you just wanted to go home and go to bed was a particular injustice.

We drank old-fashioneds with a giant square of ice and maraschino cherries. They went down easily. We kept the conversation light, and for a moment we slipped back into a world that didn't exist anymore, one where we'd meet up after work and slug a few cocktails and complain about our bosses and direct-reports with equal vitriol. The jokes got funnier as the night progressed. We'd then sober up at a new restaurant that was getting all the buzz, and we'd eventually head home, where we'd finish the night off proper—that's if the common excuse of exhaustion and an early morning conference call didn't interfere. As if sensing that we were reverting to our old habits, and not wanting to proceed to the horizontal part, Claire changed the subject.

"Langford brought the deal in," she started. "And it was for a lot more than what Carmen told you."

"I figured."

"We got a good portion of the required vouchers from that transaction alone. That and the Deakins property."

"That was my co-manager, Paul Darbin," I reminded her, although she didn't need it.

"When's he going to cut that ponytail?"

"I was hoping he'd get arrested as one of those Occupy Wall Street protesters when he went out for his lunch."

"One can dream."

"How many deals did Langford bring in?" I asked.

"Just the Carmen deal. He was working Deakins but, well, you know what happened there."

"How'd you get the rest of the vouchers?"

"We work with more brokers than just Langford. It's better to spread the work around. If it's limited to just a few they start to think they can exert pressure on the price. We prefer to keep the fear factor high. Having them constantly looking over their shoulders to see if a competitor is going to take a chunk of their kill helps us keep the costs down." Lawyers preferred hunting analogies, despite the fact that the majority of attorneys wouldn't know how to shoot a gun if given the opportunity.

"How much information do you give these brokers?"

"On what we're doing? Just enough to get what we need but not enough to screw us over with."

"So no one would know where they were actually going to build the Arroyo?"

"Some didn't even know that it was Valenti on the buying end. The sharper, more experienced brokers knew, of course."

"Was Langford one of the sharp ones?"

"He was."

"Did Carmen know?"

"I doubt it."

I recalled the name of the buyer on the buildings on Holcomb Street. Mike was able to track down the name Salas to a PO box in the Valley, but from there it was a dead end. We'd assumed it was just another shell company owned by Valenti to throw any speculators off his scent. I asked Claire about the name Salas.

"I know all the names of his shell companies, but I never heard of that one," she said. "Who are they?"

"They bought an entire block of apartment buildings near the Deakins. Temekian and his thugs pressured the owners into selling, so we assumed they were connected to Valenti."

"We didn't do any occupancy deals with them. That much I know. It sounds to me like someone heard about our interest in the occupancy vouchers and bought up some land thinking that's where the development was going. Speculation can be a risky game."

"So the Arroyo is not being built anywhere near the Deakins."

She shook her head rather than replying verbally. I was treading on an area that was very dangerous for

Claire. We had already gone over a level past "confidential" and were entering territory that could very well ruin her career if it got out that she'd given me this information. For someone who cared as much about her career as she did, this could not have been an easy thing to agree to.

"Don't worry," I said. "I'll be discreet with the information you're giving me."

"Discreet with what?" she asked.

That was when she pulled an envelope out of her bag and slid it over to me. Later that evening, when I had time to peruse the envelope's contents, I realized that it contained all the voucher transactions involved in the Arroyo project. It also included information on the actual site of the new concept mall. It was going to be much farther north from the Deakins, close to the actual arroyo for which it was named. It was to abut a row of Victorian mansions, now under the care of a historical society that served as the sole reminder of the area's celebrated past. Claire had chosen to photocopy all of the documents to eliminate any kind of electronic trail. At the bar I simply tucked it into my bag, like we were two spies passing state secrets.

"These things are hitting me already," Claire said as she downed the last drops of her drink.

"One more?"

"Then what?" she asked.

I knew what she was referring to. That old routine was hovering around us. Dusk and sweetened whiskey and jukebox standards were conspiring against us. We bathed in a pleasant melancholy in which neither of us wanted to be alone.

"Bourbon makes me nostalgic," she said. "I gotta fight it."

We settled up and stumbled out onto the street, where the next generation waited patiently in line for the hand-off. The evening traffic was beginning to die down, and there was a chill that seemed to come from above and pool around us. I walked Claire back to her car in a lot a few blocks away. We were in a quiet corner of the near-empty expanse of asphalt. We hugged and she put her arms underneath my coat and I felt her cold hands through my shirt. She buried her face into my neck, and I felt her warm breath on my skin.

"I miss you," she said, but not in a way that meant come back.

RIALTO

fucking hate cops," the man grunted, stuffing the rest of his Dodger Dog in his mouth.

In the middle half of the third inning, the public address announcer had invited all of us to stand and honor five heroes from the Los Angeles Police Department, the LA County Sheriffs, and Glendale PD. Cheli was the only woman among the bunch. She was awarded the Medal of Heroism in part for her conduct in the Temekian affair. A bunch of suits shook hands and posed for photographs as they pinned a ribbon on the lapel of her blazer. Cheli was only one of five honorees, but she clearly held sway in the group. When it was her time to get the award, the other recipients applauded.

I'd called her to discuss the recent developments regarding the vouchers. That's when she told me about the ceremony and that I should come and we could talk it over there. From my seat I could see her beaming. I knew how much it meant to her. To stand among this group of men was probably more enjoyable to her than whatever medal she added to her curio cabinet.

The group of heroes was quickly shuttled off the field so the game could continue. I left my seat and headed back to the ramp. A few fans approached the officers and shook their hands. The public's attitude toward the police was polarized—it was either unfaltering respect or outright hatred.

I hovered nearby to allow for more photographs, handshakes, and pats on the back. I noticed an older Latina standing to my right. Outfitted in a cheap dress and sandals, she patiently watched the proceedings. I found myself intrigued by this woman, who clearly wasn't here for the game. She flinched when the computer-generated clapping blared from speakers overhead. Each time she cupped both hands over her ears until it stopped. She looked like she was heading to a church social, and probably was by the look of the bulge in her handbag, about the size of a Bible.

The glad-handing show was nearly complete, and Cheli and I made eye contact. She smiled and waved me over. I gave her a quick hug and she took my arm and led me over to the older woman.

"Chuck, this is my mom, Efigenia."

I studied her up close. She had dark, tired eyes and lids that struggled to stay open. Her sandals were too small and the sides of her feet, heavily calloused from much walking, spilled over the edges. Her perfume smelled like the lobby of a convalescent home. There was a resemblance to Cheli somewhere in the color of her eyes and bump in her nose, but I'd always thought seeing resemblances like that was a trick our minds played on us. If told two strangers were sisters, you'd find similarities between the two that didn't exist.

"It's nice to meet you," I said to the old woman. "You must be very proud of your daughter."

Efigenia nodded and stood there quietly looking around at all the people. By the expression on her face, this wasn't a place she wanted to be. She clutched at her purse with both hands like it was her only worldly possession.

"Pretty good show out there," I said to Cheli, flicking the medal on her lapel. "And a nice little piece of hardware."

"Thanks," she said. "Let's go up to the Stadium Club. They're holding a reception for us." We made a move toward the elevator, but her mom didn't follow. "Come on, Mom, there's a party upstairs. They have a buffet."

Efigenia stood her ground. She said something to Cheli in Spanish. I didn't understand it but I could read the body language. Her mother wasn't interested in the party.

"Just for a little bit. It will be fun," she pleaded cheerily.

Again the woman responded in Spanish. What was communicated clearly irritated Cheli. She pursed her lips, trying to contain her frustration. "I think he can manage to make his own dinner this one time," she said.

The woman was immovable. Every plea in English was met with a Spanish dismissal, and with each exchange Cheli grew more frustrated and her mother more intractable, gripping that handbag harder and harder like it was a rescue line.

"This is great, Mom. Thanks for all the support. Just once you'd think you could be there for me and share in my success. It's okay," she said brightly but not masking her true feelings. "It doesn't bother me. It's not like I'm missing anything that was there before. You see how it is," she turned to me and spoke as if the old woman were no longer there. "Remember I told you about Latino families? You said all families are that way, but seriously, can you imagine your own mother acting like this?"

She laughed shrilly, and I felt sorry for her. Her voice was at a pitch to draw the attention of those around us, and the gawkers got a free show while they waited in line for their beer. "But what do you expect from someone who didn't feel the need to come to her own daughter's wedding? Everyone was too good for Don, but nobody had any problem living in the house he paid for. No doubt El Principe didn't have any issue sitting on his fat ass for free."

Cheli had reached a point of hysteria in which resignation overrode her feelings of anger toward her mother. Her voice got soft, quiet, almost sing-songy. "All these years, all the sacrifices, all the things I had to do." She found her composure and managed a smile. "I am going to go upstairs and enjoy myself like I should. I can't help it if you don't want to come."

She turned and joined a group of people heading upstairs to the party. I stayed behind, as did her mother. The old woman loosened her grip on her purse and slowly headed for the exit. I gave her a few moments then followed her out the same gate. Playing over in my head was the same line, "all the things I had to do."

❉ ❉ ❉

I couldn't risk trying to find my car in the expansive parking lot. If I did, there was no way I could loop back and locate Cheli's mother. Near the gate's exit, I spotted a line of black cars whose drivers were whiling away the time. A lot of corporate guys hired cars to drive them to the game so they could get loaded and not have to worry about driving home. I approached one of the drivers and offered him three hundred bucks to drive me. He was an older black man with watery eyes and a permanent sheen like skin fresh out of a hot shower.

"How long and how far?" he replied.

I told him I didn't know, but if we didn't make it back by the time the game was over, I'd double his fee.

"Hop in," he said.

I instructed the driver to follow Efigenia from a short distance. I didn't know where her car was parked and didn't want to lose her out of the several exits off the plateau. The driver was tickled with his assignment.

"Never did a tail job before," he said with a smile.

Dodger Stadium's parking lot was a blooming flower emanating from the bud of the ballpark. The various parking sections were layered on top of two arterial roads that ringed the stadium. The roads eventually led to the main stem that funneled cars inside from Sunset Boulevard.

"She park in the last row?" the driver asked out loud and soon got an answer. Efigenia limped her way across the hot asphalt toward the outer layer of parking sections marked by letters deep into the alphabet. But she didn't stop there. She crossed the last section and continued on past the ticket booths and down the hill to Sunset. Three times she had to pause to catch her breath. The driver and I shared the same guilty feeling of watching an old woman struggle while we sat idly a safe distance behind her.

"This isn't as much fun as I thought it would be," he said.

She waited at a bus stop on Sunset while we parked across the street from her. We sat there for nearly an hour before an express bus arrived.

"Let's see where it takes us," I instructed the driver.

We followed it through a numbing number of stops along Cesar Chavez before the express bus finally turned into its namesake and merged onto the freeway heading east out of the city toward San Bernardino. I placed a call to Detective Ricohr.

"You're still at it?" he asked.

"As you are," I answered.

Ricohr didn't acknowledge that remark directly.

"Lots of loose ends on this one," he admitted.

"I have an idea on tying some up."

"Is that right?"

"But I need your help."

I explained what I wanted him to do. He didn't reject my request, but he didn't jump all over it either.

"I'll see what I can do," he said. "You sure about this?"

I told him the truth. "I'm pretty sure."

There was a long pause and then he said, "Good enough for me."

I hung up, leaned my head against the seat, and enjoyed the crisp chill of the sedan's air conditioning. It felt like it was going to be a long ride. Outside my window scrolled a landscape of relentless urban sprawl. Leaving Los Angeles by freeway robbed you of the satisfaction of escape. Unlike other cities, there was no light-switch moment on the way out of town when the urban chaos decisively converted into suburban tranquility. The parts outside Los Angeles felt remarkably similar to the ones inside, except the buildings had the luxury of being placed a foot or two farther apart, which at seventy miles per hour was impossible to discern.

The bus led us into the Inland Empire. To the north the mountains loomed overhead through a pink-gray haze. Below was a flat expanse latticed with high-tension wires and concrete freeways. There was little natural shade in this area. Numerous times we crossed mile-wide gullies piled with boulders from the range above and now bleached bone-white in the relentless summer sun. As we passed San Bernardino, we started to see the developments.

From a distance, entire swaths of land were covered in a terra-cotta canopy, a result of the near-ubiquitous use of the same petroleum-engineered roofing tiles. The developments that blanketed the area rolled effortlessly from hill to hill and were corralled by high walls demarcating where the community ended and the virgin land began. Everything was washed in earth tones—ochre and slate and sand—but there was nothing natural about it. Each development felt like it was manufactured elsewhere and plopped randomly in this random stretch of land.

The houses behind the stucco walls were laid out with orange-grove symmetry and placed so tightly together that you and your neighbor could read off the same morning newspaper. All the homes had the same design: a two-story, 2,600-square-foot manse comprising four bedrooms, two and a half baths, and an open floor plan with the additional features of a two-car garage, dual-paned windows, and double-hung doors. The original designer of these homes had a thing for even numbers. The names of the developments sounded Italian or Spanish, but were neither. As with every other element in the community, they were designed to recall a Mediterranean Eden. The developers sold the bliss of the Southern European countryside to people who had never traveled farther east than Las Vegas. The developments had just enough ironwork, stone fountains, and gravel courtyards to evoke the atmosphere of a "villa" but without the risk of getting sued for false advertising.

The express bus pulled off the highway into one of the first developments in the area. A giant sign announcing the entrance to the Rialto spanned a four-lane road. Efigenia exited the bus and made her way through one of the small gates. We gave her some space and then followed a safe distance behind her.

I marveled at the emptiness. There were no children in sight and very little activity at all. Homes with for-sale signs outnumbered homes without them. Every third driveway had a car parked in it. The rest were empty. Yellowing newspapers piled up on doorsteps because the owners hadn't bothered to cancel their subscriptions. Lawns were unmowed, and the desert hardscape crept out from underneath. They'd kept the wild at bay with their towering walls but once the spigot was turned off, the land quickly reverted to its natural state.

This was the epicenter of the housing crisis. While Los Angeles took a haircut during the housing bust, San Bernardino County took its cut at the knees. To the thousands of people who bought into that Mediterranean dream through the magic of no money down and

the negative amortization mortgage, this was a hope-
less proposition. The entire area was drowning in underwater mortgages. Even those few who still had jobs
and could afford their monthly payments were facing
twenty years of never recouping what they'd paid for
their homes. The bright ones just walked away, and so
the vicious cycle continued.

Efigenia concluded her long journey at one of these
nameless houses quite indistinguishable from the rest.
She plodded up the walkway and went inside. I told the
driver to pull over at the corner and instructed him to
come back in twenty minutes. Before he could say anything, I gave him a hundred dollars to assuage his fear
that all this had been one big swindle to get a free ride
out to San Berdoo.

I gave it a few minutes before approaching the
house. It was unnervingly quiet out there. The sun felt
hotter than back in Los Angeles. I was already sweat-
ing, and my arms began to itch in the heat. I rang the
bell and anxiously waited on the front stoop. At last the
front door opened and a middle-aged man blinked at
me through the screen door.

"Mr. Salas?" I asked.

EL PRINCIPE AND HIS COURT

Yeah?"

Cheli's brother was about my height but with a pronounced pot belly and cheeks that were beginning to resemble jowls. He had a couple of old tattoos on his arms where the ink was bleeding into the skin, making it difficult to read the lettering.

"I work with your sister," I told him.

"Oh yeah? You a cop, too?"

"No." I laughed. "I'm not on the force. I do contract work with them. Anyway, Cheli was talking up this area. She said there's a lot of homes you can buy up cheap, so I thought I'd drive out here and check it out for myself."

"Cheap, you don't know cheap. Half this shit's empty. It's like a ghost town, man."

"Yeah, it looks that way. How long have you lived here?"

"In this house?" he said and thought it over. "Not even a month. We've been bouncing around."

"Is that right? Where were you before that?" I tried to keep it breezy and not make it feel like an inquisition.

"Let's see. We were over in Covina for a few months then we had to get out of there. We stayed with some cousins for a while." I remembered the night Mike was killed, the last thing he said was that he wanted to check up on a lead out in Covina but wanted to wait until traffic died down. "Before that we had the back unit in Azusa after we lost the house in Rosemead."

"That's a lot of bouncing around."

"No doubt. My sister and her crazy real estate deals. She always got something going and always got us moving somewhere. What she don't understand is it's hard on me and my mom. I take care of my mom. She's getting old and needs the help, you know. I take her to the doctor and her appointments, but it's hard when we keep moving."

"Sounds like she's got a good son," I said. He liked that. In his self-absorbed delusions, the Prince who had been taken care of all his life started to believe he was the caretaker. I wondered how the money worked. I was certain Cheli was the main source of funding for this household but wanted to confirm it. "Must be hard finding work out here," I commiserated.

"Me, I'm on disability so I can't really work. But it's tough, bro. Money don't go very far." Far enough to buy this house, I thought. El Principe was looking more and more like a harmless rube, completely oblivious to the chaos going on around him. His name was on the deeds to properties that were at the root of four murders, and he didn't seem to know anything about it. "You know, an Armenian friend of mine was also talking about this area. His name is Temekian. Ardavan Temekian." I waited for any kind of reaction. I got none. "Do you know him?"

"He doesn't know any of them," I heard a voice behind me.

Cheli stood on the walk. Her eyes were shielded behind dark shades, and she still had the ribbon from the ceremony pinned to her lapel. In her other hand she casually held a gun by her side.

"Why are we out here talking? Let's all go inside," she suggested. I didn't have much of a choice. I quickly glanced down the street but didn't see the car or my driver.

"Where's your car?" she asked. "Did you come with someone?"

"Yeah, but I don't see him."

She thought it over. "Maybe he'll show up later."

We went inside and Cheli motioned for me to sit on the couch while she hung by the front door. The room was sparsely decorated. It didn't look like they used more than two or three rooms in the house. There was nothing permanent about the space—no pictures on the walls, the TV haphazardly placed on a couple of milk crates. There were still moving boxes stacked in the corner as if in anticipation of another frantic uprooting. From the other room came the sounds and smells of Efigenia preparing dinner.

"My mom's making posole if you guys want to stay for dinner," El Principe offered. The poor woman had barely gotten home before having to slave away in the kitchen.

"We're fine," Cheli answered.

El Principe wasn't all that sharp, but he quickly picked up on the tension between Cheli and me and quietly shuffled out of the room. As soon as he was gone, I turned to Cheli.

"Why did you kill them?"

Cheli gave me the once-over.

"Lift up your shirt and turn around," she instructed. She wanted to make sure I wasn't wearing a wire. I did as requested and sat back down. "How did you say you got out here?"

"I told you, someone drove me."

"Who did?"

"I paid a car service."

"All the way out here? Where is he?"

"I don't know."

Cheli called out to her mother in the next room. Efigenia appeared in the doorway and wiped her hands with an old rag. Cheli spoke to her in Spanish, but her mother barely seemed to listen. The old woman kept wiping her hands with the rag despite the fact they were already dry. Cheli rattled off a string of instructions but the faster she spoke the more her mother began shaking her head. The old woman stared blankly at the soiled carpet. Whatever Cheli was pitching, Efigenia wanted no part of it.

"Listen to me for once," she told her mother. "We have to get out of here!"

Efigenia finally had enough. She dismissed her daughter with a condescending wave of the towel and returned to the kitchen to finish dinner.

"They never get it," Cheli ranted to herself. "Why am I the only one who tries to make things better? They just sit here and accept it as if this were all there is." She gestured to the less-than-modest living room. "Like they don't deserve better."

"They seem happy, Cheli."

"Content," she countered, "but not happy. And don't lecture me. Maybe you had it easy, but I've scratched for everything I got. I scratched for them and for that one big payday so I wouldn't have to scratch anymore."

"There is no payoff. Valenti isn't going to build anywhere near those properties you own. They're worthless, just like they were before you bought them." She stopped pacing and studied me as I continued. "Langford played you. He let you think Valenti was going to build the next concept mall by the Deakins Building, but they're breaking ground ten miles up the road near South Pas. All Langford wanted from you was help securing the vouchers."

"What vouchers?" she asked. I walked through all the details regarding the occupancy vouchers. The pain of the realization that she had been duped started to show on her face. In an odd way, I felt sorry for her. She sat down on a rocking chair by the door and stared vacantly at the floor.

"I imagine it all started with Ed," I continued. "Langford needed to close on the Deakins but Ed balked. Langford didn't tell you the reason, but I imagine it was because Ed had found out about the treasure trove of vouchers he was sitting on and wanted to get paid for them. So Langford calls you in to apply some pressure. Maybe you'd done this sort of thing in the past for him when he and your husband were working deals. And you certainly had the contacts in the Armenian community who could put some fear into Ed to get him to shut up and accept the original offer. It got out of control and I guess we'll never know who actually pulled the trigger—you or Temekian. The call Ed made to the Glendale

Police the day he died makes sense now. I thought it was because he was worried, but he was actually calling you. He didn't know what he was walking into that night."

I took a moment to gauge her condition. It was hard to read so I pressed on.

"At this point you got greedy. Langford was purposely hazy about the details behind the Arroyo. He didn't want you to know where they were actually going to build the mall because you might make things difficult for him. But you saw a big payday. As soon as they break ground, values on the homes right around it will skyrocket. And so you bought up some properties—with the help of Temekian's muscle—before the news got out that the next, great Valenti creation was opening up in Lincoln Heights.

"What was the deal—you get Temekian to apply a little Armenian mob pressure in exchange for scuttling whatever investigation was on him at the time? At first his arrest confused me. If you two were working together, why would you bring him in? But then I figured it out—it was a warning. You didn't want him cutting any deals. If he stuck to the plan, you wouldn't feed him to the wolves. But that was the plan all along—make him the fall guy.

"Only problem was Temekian was no dummy. He saw it coming and approached me first. I wondered why he was so afraid of the police that he wanted an intermediary. He wasn't afraid of the police as much as he was afraid of you. Poor guy didn't know we had a relationship. He thought I set him up when you confronted him at the motel. He died thinking I had a hand in sealing his fate."

That part hurt—that someone went to his grave believing in his heart that I had betrayed him. That and the needless death of my friend.

"Why did you kill Mike?"

"Because he found out about them," she answered dully, motioning to her mother and brother obliviously eating their dinner in the room next to us. "I overheard him mention Covina and knew what it meant. I tried to head him off but it was too late."

Then it made sense why Mike died where he did, the way he did.

"You pulled him over with the siren. Why else would he get off the freeway in that part of town and casually wait with his window down for someone to approach his car? He thought it was the CHP nabbing him for speeding."

"If we walk out that front door, will there be police?"

I laughed. It was the first response that came to me. "You're not even listening to me. It's over. It's all over—"

"Shut up!" she snapped, and the gun jerked up and pointed right at me. She stood over me and looked down at me over the sight of the gun. "I asked you if there will be police."

"I don't know."

"Stand up," she said coolly, and for the first time since I entered that house I was convinced she was going to shoot me. Nothing significantly had changed— her voice was the same, the look in her eyes was the same, her demeanor was unchanged. It just felt like my death was close by.

"I asked Detective Ricohr to run a test on the gun you planted by Temekian. The one they found in the alley—the one you put there. You went back to your car and got it while I stayed by the body. Ricohr's going to see if it's the same gun that your husband used to kill himself."

"Don's gun?" she whispered.

"It will link you to the three murders."

"Don's gun?" she said again. I started to see fissures forming in her fragile shell. Her eyes darted erratically across the room. "No one ever liked Don," she said sadly and with a great release, like a giant exhale came over her and the room. Something ended in that moment. "All we wanted was to make something of ourselves," she added as the gun fell harmlessly by her side. Cheli looked at me with peace in her eyes.

"I tried," she said.

Cheli walked out of the living room and into the kitchen. I heard a door in the back open and then rattle shut. And then I heard nothing more.

SMILE NOW, CRY LATER

Yucaipa Police found her car the following day during a routine patrol of a small industrial complex just off the freeway. Cheli was in the driver's seat. She had a single gunshot wound to the head, and her body was propped up by the seatbelt, which remained fastened. There was no note.

For the second time I was sequestered in my Lincoln Heights apartment while the details were ironed out. The county of Los Angeles wasn't in the business of prosecuting dead people for the crimes they committed; there were too many living defendants to worry about. As a result, the four murders linked to Cheli went unsolved. That wasn't to say the police hadn't built a strong case against her. Detective Ricohr had had his suspicions all along but was never able to tie anything directly to her. He did follow up on my request to link the gun that killed Easy Mike and the one that Cheli's ex-husband used. They came back a match, and the police left it at that.

Across the way, Glendale's force faced quite a

backlash in the press for having someone deep within their ranks involved in such heinous crimes. A few fringe groups dusted off old gripes and called for reforms, but the requests went unanswered. As far as scandals went, this one had little impact. The public didn't seem to mind. For them it was more a confirmation of a long-held opinion than anything else. The Glendale force was always dirty, and this just further proved it. It was, after all, difficult to besmirch an already-blackened reputation. As they had done in the past, the Glendale PD bided its time until the chatter dissipated and everyone moved onto another story.

I never knew what happened to Cheli's mom or brother. After calling the police, I left them as they were, at the table quietly eating their dinner and completely oblivious to the chaos that surrounded their lives. They never showed much interest in Cheli's rise, and they showed equal disinterest in her downfall.

One day close to the holidays I ran into Detective Ricohr in Little Tokyo. We hadn't spoken in months. We talked mostly about the weather and almost nothing about the case. We made a promise to meet up for lunch sometime, knowing that it was just a pleasantry and that we'd never actually try to find the time. Surprisingly, two days later I got a call from him.

"How about we meet for that lunch?"

We met at a sandwich shop near my office. Before we could get past even hellos, he plopped a giant accordion folder on the table. It was the case file.

"I can't let you take it with you but I can disappear for an hour while you look through it."

I studied the giant folder.

"Why'd you bring this?"

"You seem like a guy who wants some answers."

He was a good detective. Much like Easy Mike had a desire to know the details behind his father's death, I had this need to try to understand Cheli's final day. I wanted some sort of narrative to ground what was otherwise a senseless waste of people's lives.

"Last week I drove out to the lot where they found her car," I said.

"Why'd you do that?"

"I'm not sure," I answered truthfully. I had stood in the flat, desolate parking lot for three hours searching for any kind of detail to latch onto that would provide even a hint of motivation for the destructive path she had taken leading up to that final act when she took her life. We're always looking for order in the chaos.

"Did you find anything?" he asked.

"No."

There was nothing poignant in Cheli's death. It would have been cleaner if the gun that had killed her husband, Ed Vadaresian, Langford, and my friend Mike was the same one that took her life, but that gun was some seventy miles away locked in a police evidence locker. She instead used her service revolver, the same one that murdered Ardavan Temekian.

I studied the folder and its bulging contents, but I no longer wanted to know what was inside. More scraps of information weren't going to satisfy what was gnawing at me. "It's okay," I told Detective Ricohr, "I don't want to know the details."

The Arroyo broke ground on a hot Wednesday morning the following year. There was the usual uproar from the South Pas neighborhood council over congestion issues, but Valenti was able to ram this one through. A lot of that had to do with the secrecy behind the project. Despite the information I had stirred up, the location and announcement of the development surprised residents and gave them little time to rally their troops against it. Plus, everyone in this city likes malls.

There was no uproar over Carmen Hernandez's women's center, which started construction with little fanfare about six months later—public money always took longer to fund than the private sector's. Her project was in a neighborhood that no one who mattered really knew or cared much about, and thus there was no opposition, despite the fact that taxpayer money paid for it.

The Arroyo ceremony was covered on the local evening news, all twenty seconds of it. Valenti opted for cornerstone symbolism rather than the shiny shovel routine. He traced the name of his latest conquest into a just-poured, ceremonial concrete pillar. Behind him, McIntyre clapped enthusiastically like a mother at a children's beauty pageant. Everyone in the shot looked extremely proud of their achievement. Just off camera a lackey with a dampened towel waited to clean off Valenti's hands.

I didn't see Claire in the brief footage they showed, but I knew she was there, as we had been speaking more regularly for several months. The words "quick" and "amicable" aren't often used to describe a divorce, but Claire and I managed to achieve both. We got together and handled it all ourselves. It was the right thing to do—at least that's what everyone said—but it still felt awful. We split the assets evenly. She got to keep the house in Beachwood Canyon, so I guess she got the better end of the deal, but it really didn't bother me. It was already more her house than mine.

Some weeks later I decided it was time to finally leave Lincoln Heights and end my self-imposed exile. I purchased a modest house in Eagle Rock and set out plans to "kick-start" my life (a new associate who was a Harley-Davidson enthusiast had recently infused the workplace with a slew of motorcycle analogies). But like those prisoners who dread their pending release, the thought of leaving the apartment in Lincoln Heights filled me with a quiet sorrow that grew more distinct as the final day approached.

During my final week in the apartment, I was loading up the car for another run to my new home when I ran into my neighbor working on his truck. After all those months, I was finally able to put a face to the music I listened to every night. He was a lot younger than I expected, maybe in his late twenties. He had a perfectly shaved head and wore a Dodger game jersey unbuttoned to show off a mosaic of tattoos. It was a common look among cholos, so common as to border on cliché—the Old English script, the names of several people close to the bearer, some with their too-short lives recalled by birth and death years underneath their names.

He also had a stylized version of the Greek comedy and tragedy masks that took up almost an entire side of his neck. I remembered Cheli telling me that it represented the life they lived. Everything was certain to end badly—prison or death or both—so why not live it up when you are young and deal with the consequences later?

"You moving?" he asked. I was always disappointed when people spoke to me in English in a predominantly Latino neighborhood. Just once I wanted to feel like I belonged.

"Yeah, tomorrow's my last day."

"Good luck, man," he said and ducked back under the hood.

"Are you the one who plays the oldies every night?" I asked.

He sort of smiled and acknowledged it was he.

"Why do you only play the sad ones?"

"I only play the good ones," he corrected.

I nodded. The best ones always were the saddest.

"Still depressing, though," I said with a laugh.

"Sometimes," he started, "it's good to be sad. I lived the crazy life when I was a kid." To me he was still a kid. "I did some things, a lot of things, that I'm paying for now. And I sort of need to be reminded of that, so I like to get all sad at night. But then I get my girl with me and we dance and she sort of makes it right again." He looked suddenly embarrassed about sharing so much detail with a stranger. "That probably don't make no sense to you," he said apologetically.

"Makes a lot of sense," I told him.

"What's your favorite?" he asked. "I can add it to the list."

"*In the Still of the Night.*"

"I'll put it in the mix."

"Sounds good," I lied.

Unlike him, I didn't have anyone to help me make things right again. I made a note to be good and drunk and fast asleep by the time the music started.

About the Author

Adam Walker Phillips is a twenty-year veteran of corporate America. He has endured countless PowerPoint decks, offsite retreats and visioning sessions, synergies, and synergistically minded cross-functional teams, all to bring you the Chuck Restic mystery series. He lives with his wife and children in Los Angeles.